# The Beemaster's Cottage

### De-ann Black

Toffee
Apple

Toffee Apple Publishing

Other books in the Cottages, Cakes & Crafts book series are:

Book 1 - The Flower Hunter's Cottage.
Book 2 - The Sewing Bee by the Sea.
Book 3 - The Beemaster's Cottage.
Book 4 - The Chocolatier's Cottage
Book 5 - The Bookshop by the Seaside
Book 6 - The Dressmaker's Cottage

Published by Toffee Apple Publishing 2015

The Beemaster's Cottage

ISBN: 9781520773650

Toffee
Apple
Toffee Apple Publishing

Also by De-ann Black (Romance, Action/Thrillers & Children's books). See her Amazon Author page or website for further details about her books, screenplays, illustrations, art and fabric designs.
www.De-annBlack.com

## Romance:

The Sewing Shop
Heather Park
The Tea Shop by the Sea
The Bookshop by the Seaside
The Sewing Bee
The Quilting Bee
Snow Bells Wedding
Snow Bells Christmas
Summer Sewing Bee
The Chocolatier's Cottage
Christmas Cake Chateau
The Beemaster's Cottage
The Sewing Bee By The Sea
The Flower Hunter's Cottage

The Christmas Knitting Bee
The Sewing Bee & Afternoon Tea
The Vintage Sewing & Knitting Bee
Shed In The City
The Bakery By The Seaside
Champagne Chic Lemonade Money
The Christmas Chocolatier
The Christmas Tea Shop & Bakery
The Vintage Tea Dress Shop In Summer
Oops! I'm The Paparazzi
The Bitch-Proof Suit

## Action/Thrillers:

Love Him Forever.
Someone Worse.
Electric Shadows.

The Strife Of Riley.
Shadows Of Murder.

## Children's books:

Faeriefied.
Secondhand Spooks.
Poison-Wynd.

Wormhole Wynd.
Science Fashion.
School For Aliens.

## Colouring books:

Summer Garden. Spring Garden. Autumn Garden. Sea Dream.
Festive Christmas. Christmas Garden. Flower Bee. Wild Garden.
Faerie Garden Spring. Flower Hunter. Stargazer Space. Bee Garden.

## Embroidery books:

Floral Nature Embroidery Designs
Scottish Garden Embroidery Designs

# Contents

# CHAPTER ONE

## Scottish Seaside Summer

'Oh, look at his lovely blue eyes. They match his cable knit jumper. I love that pattern.' Ethel admired the handsome male model in the knitting magazine. She was reading the new magazines in the post office along with her friend, Hilda.

Hilda, looked at him. 'I'm not one for fancying men with sandy hair, but for him I'd make an exception.'

Ethel nodded. 'He's all windswept and rugged. There's something about him that reminds me of the beemaster. I know Bredon's blond and a bit more refined, but there's an air of gorgeousness about them.'

Ethel and Hilda, both in their retirement years, hadn't changed since the last time I'd seen them. Four years had passed and Ethel's silvery blonde hair had lost none of its sparkle. Hilda had no more or less grey within her brown hair, and still appeared to be fit and strong.

They were so busy admiring the male model in the latest issue of the magazine that they didn't notice me coming into the post office. It doubled as a grocery shop. There was a grocery shop beside the post office, but out of habit from the past, I'd ventured in here to buy fresh milk and bread to take with me to the cottage. It was the first time I'd stepped inside for four years. During the past few weeks, while moving into the cottage and having my things transported from my flat in London to the Scottish Highlands, I'd done my shopping in the nearest city, keeping my distance from the likes of Ethel and Hilda until I was ready to tell them why I was back and what I was up to.

I put the grocery items down on the counter and wondered what the postmaster's reaction would be when he saw me. He was busy labelling parcels and stuffing them into bags ready for uplift.

'Well, I never expected to see you here again.' He didn't disguise his surprise. He didn't smile either. 'Are you here on holiday, Aurora? Back at the cottage for a wee break?'

'No, I'm moving back into the cottage.'

1

By now, Ethel and Hilda had darted behind the tinned soups and biscuit display. I felt their eyes boring into me, peering at me over the chocolate digestives.

He blinked. 'Moving back? To live here? I thought you'd made a whole fancy lifestyle for yourself down in London working for a glossy magazine.'

'I did, but now I'm relocating to make a new fancy lifestyle for myself here.'

'What are you going to do here? I mean, the cottage your grandfather owned is a holiday let. It must be what...four years since you left? Where are you going to stay? At the cottage? What about the holidaymakers? What about a job? Are you going to run it as a bed and breakfast? It doesn't seem your style, if you don't mind me asking.'

Yes, I was definitely back where there was no filter in the questions people asked. I'd have to get used to their ways again. Although I'd been friendly with work colleagues at the sewing, knitting and craft magazines I'd edited in London, I'd always felt like an outsider. London was a city of strangers. Some friendly strangers. Perhaps I hadn't let anyone in to get close to me. To know me. The real me. Whoever that was. Hopefully it was the woman who was back to where she'd been brought up, to live in the old cottage which had been refurbished as a holiday let. Home again. Not that I expected a warm welcome. Quite the opposite. I knew what they thought of me. Sometimes, I agreed with them. I was a magnet for trouble. Mostly unintentional.

I could hear Ethel and Hilda holding their breath, desperate to chip in. I sighed heavily. Best get it over with. 'You can stop holding your tongues, ladies. I can see you hiding behind the digestives.'

They stepped into view. Hilda's cardigan was buttoned up tight, while Ethel's shawl, hand knitted from her own yarn no doubt, sat around her shoulders. They hadn't changed. Not at all. The sun was burning a hole through the cloudless blue sky, and they were still wearing their woollies. To be fair, the sea breeze could be brisk, but walking from where I'd parked my car beside the harbour esplanade, the air was warm.

Hilda's expression was as tight as the buttons on her cardigan. She glared at me.

2

Ethel spoke first. 'Aurora,' she said, making it sound like poison. 'So, the rumours are true. We heard you were back.'

'I am.'

'What are you going to be up to?' said Hilda. 'I heard it was going to be some sort of magazine.'

'I'm launching a new magazine,' I told them.

Ethel's eyes widened. 'A magazine? Here? What kind of magazine? This is a wee community. Not many folk round here will buy it.'

I fought the urge to snap at them. 'A sewing, knitting and craft magazine. An online magazine that's filled with sewing and knitting patterns that readers can download. And lots of crafts — papercraft and —'

Their noses screwed up.

'It sounds awful fanciful,' the postmaster commented. 'Who is going to write it?'

'I'm going to write a lot of it to begin with,' I explained. 'I've been editing and creating content for this type of publication for years. I think I have the experience needed. And I plan on asking knitters, like you Ethel, and quilters like Hilda, if they'd like to contribute patterns and features for the magazine. It'll be a monthly issue.'

'You want us to write for your magazine?' Ethel exclaimed.

'Yes. You and as many others as I can gather from around here and perhaps over on the islands.'

'For free?' said Hilda.

'To begin with. But you'll be able to promote your yarn and quilts in the magazine which should result in increased sales for both of you. I won't be twisting your arms. It'll be up to you if you want to be part of the magazine. I'm putting an advert in the post office window.' I glanced at the postmaster. 'If that's okay with you?' I took the piece of paper I'd printed with details of getting involved in the magazine and handed it to him. 'I'd like to put this up on your notice board for a couple of weeks. How much do you charge these days?'

He looked at me as if overwhelmed with all the information I'd given them. 'No charge, Aurora. I'll stick it up for you.' He rang my items through the till while Ethel and Hilda whispered anxiously.

'So, would our pictures be in the magazine?' Ethel asked.

3

'Would we need to get our hair done?' Hilda added.

'It would be up to you. If you wanted your photograph alongside your byline —'

Ethel interrupted. 'Byline?'

'Your name would be on the feature along with your knitting pattern,' I explained. 'That's how it'll be to begin with. A sort of contra deal. You write content for the magazine, and you get to promote your knitting. I've read your website, Ethel. You sell the yarn you spin and dye to customers who buy it online. And you do the same with your quilts, Hilda. I also had a sneak peek at your stalls at the summer fete recently. Your items are perfect for the readership of the magazine.'

Hilda thought it over. 'It would be like free advertising in a magazine that readers who enjoy sewing and knitting would see. I'd probably sell more quilts.'

'Exactly,' I said.

Ethel sounded interested. 'When are you starting up this magazine?'

'I've already been doing the ground work on it for a year. I've been testing the market, gathering a list of potential advertisers and crafters who are interested in writing about everything from embroidery to papercraft. But the main emphasis will be on sewing and knitting patterns with easy–to–follow instructions and plenty of photographs and illustrations. The look of the magazine will be a key to selling it. *And,*' I emphasised, 'there will be more content than adverts, and no full–page ads stuck in. All advertising will be feature–related.'

'What does that mean?' said Hilda.

'It'll look like an interesting feature while it actually promotes a particular brand or product. The page will state clearly that it's an ad–feat, an advertorial, but it'll be interesting to read.'

Hilda nodded. 'I like the sound of that.'

'Me too,' said Ethel. 'Drop by my cottage. I'll tell the other girls, including Tiree. She's a young woman like yourself. Tiree moved here earlier in the year and now runs a sewing bee from the strawberry jam cottage. We'll all have a natter over tea and cake. How about tomorrow afternoon?'

'Yes, I'll do that, Ethel. I didn't know about the sewing bee. This could be very handy.'

'The bee's become very popular. Mairead goes there now too,' said Ethel. 'Mairead's another one who is new to the area. She's a botanical illustrator. I'll invite her along for our wee chat. She might want to contribute artwork for your magazine. But don't mention about going skinny dipping with Fintry.'

I gasped, wanting to protest, but Ethel continued, 'Few brides–to–be enjoy hearing about their fiancé's past exploits with other women.'

'I wasn't skinny dipping, Ethel.'

'Always got an excuse,' the postmaster muttered.

Ethel's eyes glared right at me. 'Don't tell fibs, Aurora. We all saw you diving off the flower hunter's yacht into the sea at the harbour.'

'I was wearing silk crepe de chine,' I said. 'I'd spent a fortune on the fabric and made the dress myself for the party. Everyone was fooling around. It was just a silly whim. I was young and Fintry...well...all the women fancied him, so when he challenged me to dive off the bow of his yacht I went for it.'

'You didn't need to take all your clothes off,' Hilda said through pursed lips.

'I didn't want to ruin my dress. Can you imagine what salt water would've done to the silk?'

'At least you kept your knickers on,' Hilda relented.

'Just don't go mentioning that scandalous incident to Mairead,' said Ethel. 'I think the two of you will get on, and I'm sure she'll come along tomorrow afternoon — though I'm doubtful if Judith has forgiven you for throwing a basin of cold water over her at the Hallowe'en party at my house.'

'It was an accident, Ethel. I was trying not to step on Thimble.' This was true. Thimble was doing that playful thing cats do, winding around my ankles as I walked along. We were all dressed as witches and fairies for the party at Ethel's cottage, and she'd asked me to help carry a basin of water through so we could dook for apples while she lit the pumpkins. I'd been happy to help. Unfortunately, Thimble was in a playful mood. I was dressed as a fairy and my wings snagged on a skein of yarn on a nearby shelf. Judith jumped up to lift Thimble out of the way and we sort of clashed, resulting in the full basin of cold water being tipped over Judith's witches outfit. The black and orange dye from the crepe paper she'd used to make it

5

started to run and one of the farmers offered her his shirt while simultaneously helping her to whip off her witches outfit. It was just bad timing that his wife came through from the kitchen carrying a tray of spiders' web cupcakes and saw her husband bare–chested with his arms draped around Judith. 'Was it my fault the farmer's wife jumped to the wrong conclusion?'

Ethel shrugged and adjusted her shawl. 'They had a big falling out over it. She made him sleep in the barn for a week before everyone explained to her that it was all your fault.'

'Why is it always my fault?' I snapped.

Ethel sighed. 'Because it always is.'

'What about a man, Aurora?' the postmaster piped up. 'I don't see a wedding ring on your finger.'

'Not married. No man.' I tried to disguise the bitterness in my voice.

'What happened?' he said. 'We all thought you'd hook yourself a rich man down in London, especially with your looks.'

I hadn't applied much makeup, just a hint of lipstick and mascara to emphasise my blue eyes. My hair hung loose around my shoulders, shiny chestnut, straight and blunt cut. I wore a cotton dress, a navy print with little red and white anchors and yachts, and a pair of pumps — the type of outfit I'd wear in London when the weather was warm.

The postmaster's voice drifted back to me. 'You were always a classy lassie. You look even more like a city girl now. All sophisticated and well–groomed.'

Ethel glared at him. 'And I suppose we're not?'

'You know I'd marry you if you'd let me, Ethel,' he said. This came as no surprise to them, so I assumed their flirting game was still ongoing.

Ethel adjusted her shawl. 'I'm happy as I am, thank you,' she told him, and then said to me, 'There are some new men who've moved here since you left, so if you're looking for romance —'

'I'm not. I want to concentrate on getting the magazine up and running.' Romance had never smiled sweetly on me. In fact, I'd almost given up on men. There were few I could trust, having been cheated on, lied to and swindled out of money. No, men were off the agenda.

Ethel and Hilda continued to tell me about the local totty.

6

'There's the chocolatier who is along the coast, and Bredon the beemaster. He's in the cottage nearest Tavion,' said Ethel. 'Do you remember Tavion the flower grower?'

'Yes.'

'He's taken, but Big Sam the silversmith is still single, and I know you remember him.' Ethel gave me a cheeky wink.

'I'm not getting involved with Sam,' I said.

'You used to like him.'

'No, I made a mistake, once. You were partly responsible, Ethel.'

'Me? I didn't force the drink down your throat, Aurora.'

'I asked you — what's in this ginger wine? It tastes potent. You told me it was a new recipe with extra raspberry essence.'

'It was,' said Ethel.

'Yes,' I said, 'laced with vodka and brandy.'

'I didn't expect you to drink it like lemonade,' Ethel said to me. 'You disappeared with Big Sam out the back door of the party. We all thought you were outside canoodling, not...going all the way.'

'We didn't,' I insisted, as I had before. I'd gone further than I intended, especially with Sam. I hardly fancied him at all. It was one of those vulnerable nights when everything conspired against me, including Ethel's potent ginger wine and Sam's manly charms.

'Well at least one person will be pleased to see you back here,' said the postmaster.

'Thanks for the horrible compliment,' I told him.

'You know what I mean,' he said.

Ethel gave me a knowing look. 'You have to admit, you've always been a trouble magnet, Aurora.'

Hilda nodded.

'I'm back here to work,' I told them, 'not to meddle or get involved with any of the local men.'

'Some of them are gorgeous,' said Hilda. She held up the man in the knitting magazine. 'Even more gorgeous than him.'

'He's a heartbreaker,' I said.

'We've got one or two round here.'

'But remember, Fintry the flower hunter is taken,' Ethel added.

I picked up my bag of groceries. 'I'll drop by for a chat tomorrow afternoon, Ethel. I'll bring the format of the magazine with me, and pagination sheets so you can see what I have planned for the layout and content.'

'We'll let the others know,' said Ethel.

I smiled and left them to talk about me behind my back.

The sun shone along the harbour and the sea was a deep blue–green. It had always looked beautiful in the summer. Colourful bunting fluttered in the breeze along the esplanade.

I stood for a moment and breathed in the fresh, summer air. The long stretch of coastline hadn't altered. It still looked rugged and untamed — just like the man who glanced across at me before jumping over the wall and down on to the sand. He had blond hair and was striped to the waist. His light beige trousers sat low on his trim waistline, emphasising his honey gold tanned torso and lean muscled physique. It wasn't the flower hunter. I remembered Fintry. Handsome indeed. But this man was slightly more cocky in the way he glanced at me. Fintry was quite a serious man, deep, thoughtful. Whoever this sleek–limbed man was, he looked at me with a smile in his eyes, as if amused by something that only he knew.

Then he was gone, disappearing over the wall, leaving me wondering about him, which was possibly his intention. If he was yet another handsome game player I was all out of patience to make any moves these days.

I put my shopping in the car and drove up towards the cottage which was situated between the coast and the countryside. The white–painted cottage perched on the side of a hill overlooking the harbour and the sea. When I was little, it used to frighten me. I thought one day the cottage would topple off the hill and tumble down into the fields below. It never had, of course, but as I drove up the steep hill and parked at the side of the driveway, I felt the cottage was a bit like me, always on the edge, never quite settled.

I'd arranged for my belongings to be sent to the cottage by courier, and during the past couple of weeks I'd tried to settle in. Despite having my things around, it still felt like the holiday cottage it had been for the past four years, since I'd lost my grandfather and left to live in London. I hoped it would start to feel more like home. It was home, wasn't it? It used to be in what seemed like another life. I was back, but London had changed me, changed my perception of things. Any hint of naivety had been lost in the fast pace of London life and the competitive world of magazine work. I'd

8

left London, but it hadn't left me. Not yet. Thankfully that's exactly the attitude I needed to get my magazine project up and running.

I pulled the curtains back to let more sunlight shine in through the front window of the living room. The sea sparkled in the distance. Below me, I had a view of Tavion's house and his flower fields, and another cottage — the beemaster's cottage I assumed from what Ethel had said about it being nearest to Tavion. I saw beehives in the garden. Years ago it had been a farmer's house. Now it belonged to the beemaster. Would my cottage become known as the magazine cottage? No, it didn't have the same ring to it as the beemaster's cottage or the flower hunter's cottage, or even the chocolatier's cottage which sounded delicious.

I looked around at the living room. The cottage had been completely redecorated in light creams and pastels. It still had a fireplace, but the old mantelpiece had been replaced. The kitchen was modernised and the bathroom had a new shower unit. Both bedrooms had fitted wardrobes and every convenience added.

What I loved was the view from the front windows, over the fields from this high vantage point. The view of the sea in the distance and the islands beyond. And I liked the quietude. I could think here and make great plans. If even some of those plans panned out everything would be okay. Perhaps the postmaster was right that only Big Sam the silversmith would be glad to hear that I was back. But there seemed to be quite a few new people who had moved to the vicinity and maybe they wouldn't judge me as harshly as those in the past. All I had to do was work hard, put my plans for the magazine in action, and do my utmost not to cause trouble.

# CHAPTER TWO

## The Bee Garden

After dinner, I decided to tidy the front garden and enjoy the sunshine that was still pouring over the coastline like liquid amber.

I hadn't done any gardening since I'd lived here with my grandfather. I didn't have a garden in London.

Grandfather had worked as a fisherman all his days down at the harbour. He hadn't taught me how to garden. I'd simply picked up the basics watching and helping him. Ill–equipped to bring up a little girl, he'd taken great pride in teaching me how to box. An amateur boxer, he'd remained fit and strong until the end. My parents were a false memory and scattered photographs. Grandfather never wanted to discuss the details of why my mother left my father holding the baby and found a better life for herself. All I knew for sure was that my father swiftly left my grandfather to bring me up while he went to live in Australia. I wasn't even a year old. We never saw him again. A handful of letters from abroad during the first couple of years faded to nothing. Finally, it was just my grandfather and me. But I'd learned to give a knockout punch. Not that I envisaged using it again. An obstreperous ex–boyfriend was the last person to be on the receiving end when I found out he'd been using me as an extra bank account to fund his weekends away with his girlfriend.

I breathed in the scent of the flowers, the grass and the warmth of the early evening. There was no heavy, grimy work to be done, so I wore a summery, light blue chambray dress, the type that improves the more it's washed, until it has a vintage quality to it.

The warm air brushed against my bare arms, and I felt the pressure of my busy life lift a couple of notches from my shoulders. Suddenly, I was a young girl again, playing in my grandfather's garden after dinner, free from all the cares and woes I'd since acquired.

I picked a bunch of sweet peas, and as I selected gypsophila to go with them, I saw a black cat stroll past. A tiny silver thimble hung from its collar. It stopped and gazed at me with knowing in its green eyes.

'Thimble?'

It stood its ground for a moment and then padded on through the long strands of grass bordering the road. I watched him pause to sniff a wildflower, and then I must've blinked because he disappeared into a nearby field.

Yes, this was definitely the dressmaker's cat, whatever version. I wasn't one for myth and lore, but there had always been something different about the dressmaker and her cat. Judith and Ethel believed she was fey, and by association her cat had the gift as well. If I'd been inclined to believe this, I'd also have considered whether the cat was sent to check on me, to see if I really was back to stay.

A sudden breeze blew up from the sea. A strong wave of air caused the front door of the cottage to slam shut. I'd left the keys dangling inside the lock. I shouldn't have been locked out and yet I was. Something had juddered the lock mechanism.

I put the sweet peas down and considered my options. The kitchen door was locked, as were all the windows except the front bedroom window which was open a fraction. I reached inside and tried to flick the catch to open it wider, but it was jammed. I could only open it wide enough to squeeze through, and even that was doubtful.

Okay, I could do this. There was no one else around to see me climb ungainly through the window.

I kicked my shoes off and stepped up on to the window ledge. Rambling roses growing round the front of the house brushed against my bare legs. I squeezed my shoulders through and began to pull on the inside ledge to lever my way inside. I got halfway. I would've made it all the way if the back of my dress hadn't snagged on the window frame.

The breeze seemed to have a grudge against me because it blew the skirt of my dress up as a voice called out to me, 'Can I give you a hand there? Are you stuck?'

Oh yes, the trouble magnet was in full force. It was a man's voice. I had no idea who it was. It didn't sound like the postmaster, Fintry, Tavion or even Big Sam. I had a stranger coming to my rescue.

'I think my dress is caught on the window frame.' I tried to sound calm and authoritative. If this man intended harming me or taking advantage of the situation, for there was no doubt that my knickers were in view, I wanted to make sure he knew I wasn't the easy target I appeared to be. Hopefully, he was some sort of helpful type. People from around here tended not to be twisted rats.

My luck was in. He unhooked my dress where it had snagged and shouldered me inside the cottage. I landed in a heap on the bedroom floor, but I was in. No harm done. Shame and embarrassment didn't count.

I adjusted my dress and hurried through to the hallway. The keys needed only a slight jiggle to unlock the front door. Typical.

A man stood there, silhouetted against the evening sunlight. I hesitated longer than was socially acceptable. Wow! He was luscious — all golden blond hair, burnished tan, tall, fit looking with beautiful blue eyes and a sexy smile. His white shirt was open at the neck and the sleeves were rolled up.

And then I recognised him. The man from the harbour wall who'd stared at me as if something amused him.

He was still smiling at me.

'I saw you starting to climb through the window and thought I'd better hurry up and help.' His voice was as smooth as molten sunshine.

'Thank you. I'm not a burglar.'

He laughed, and this enhanced his handsome features even more. Jeez, he was a looker. A heartbreaker. The last type of man I needed smiling at me.

'I know who you are, sort of.' He turned and glanced down and across the fields towards the beemaster's cottage. 'I live in the cottage down there.'

'You're the beemaster?'

'You make me sound infamous.'

'Ethel and Hilda mentioned you to me.'

'All scandalous I suppose. The ladies round here tend to have vivid imaginations and a lot of time to gossip.'

'Very scandalous,' I joked with him.

'I'd love to hear the stories.'

He was fishing for an invitation to come in. I stepped aside. 'Would you like to come in for a cup of tea, coffee or a cold drink?'

He smiled again. Oh dear. I'd promised myself that men were off the agenda, at least until I was settled and had established the magazine. My stomach knotted. I hadn't felt like that for a long time.

12

'Tea, thanks.' He was inside the living room now. He extended his hand. 'I'm Bredon.'

'Aurora.'

I put the kettle on and was aware of him standing at the kitchen door, leaning casually.

I hurried to set up the cups and the teapot while I babbled on about the keys getting stuck in the lock, intending to oil it so it didn't happen again, the reasons why I was here, moving from London, my grandfather, setting up the magazine. I heard myself prattling on, spilling it all out at speed, while he stood calmly watching and listening.

I finally handed him a cup of tea.

Elegant tanned hands accepted it gratefully. 'You need to slow down.'

I blinked. 'I'm used to being busy.'

'You're busier than my bees, and summer is my busiest time.'

We went through to the living room and he wandered over to where I'd set up my laptop and magazine layouts on the table near the window.

'I have a lot of work to do for the magazine,' I said. 'I plan to slow down a bit once the first issue is launched.'

'I can understand. Setting up a new venture and moving from London and all that but...the lights are ablaze in this house every night into the early hours of the morning. Not that I've been deliberately spying on you. Don't get me wrong. And I'm not one to talk about working all hours as I'm the same at the moment. I'm busy with new hives as well as tending to the established hives. I'm often up during the night. And every night I look up, your cottage is lit up. Sometimes I've seen you standing outside in the front garden — and fighting your own shadow. I'm not sure what that's about. I almost came up to say something. To ask what was wrong.'

'There was nothing wrong. It's just...my grandfather was left to bring me up and the main thing he taught me was how to box. I used to practise in the garden with him or on my own — shadow boxing.' I sighed and revealed more than I intended. 'I guess I wanted to do what I used to do — but we can't capture the past, can we?'

'We're all built from pieces of our past. I don't see why we shouldn't use what we've learned — to try to remember how something felt. It must be strange being back here after living in

London for years, especially now you're here on your own. You must miss your grandfather.'

'I do, but if I dwell on it I'll drown in self–doubt and sink. No one's going to pull me up, except me.'

'You've got friends here surely? Ethel, Hilda —'

'They weren't entirely over the moon to see me back here. I have a reputation for causing trouble.'

'No one was sure what you were up to. The postmaster thought you were here on holiday. There were the rumours of a magazine.'

'Well, now people know. Ethel and Hilda seem eager to be part of the magazine, contributing knitting and sewing patterns.' I glanced at the pile of paperwork. 'Ethel has invited me to her cottage tomorrow afternoon to chat about it. Other women, those involved in various crafts, will be there.'

He lifted one of the pagination sheets. 'Is this how you make a magazine?'

'It's part of the process. The pagination sheets list the contents of each page. It gives a rundown of the features. It allows me to see the whole concept for the opening issue. Everything has to work with everything else.'

I reached over and pointed to a double–page spread on a layout sheet. 'On this page will be a paragraph describing a knitting pattern for a tea cosy along with the actual pattern and photographs of the finished item — including how to knit a bumblebee.'

'A bee?'

'I'm proposing a bumblebee tea cosy pattern be included in the first issue. I'm hoping Ethel or Judith will knit one. Tea cosies are always popular whatever time of year it is. I'd like them to knit a bee for the top of it instead of adding a pom pom, but we may have to go with the pom pom. It depends on what they're willing to knit.'

'You seem to have it all figured out.'

'I've been working on it for about a year. There are some items that are always popular. Knitted tea cosy patterns are one of them. Knitted softies and soft toys. Hats, scarves, mitts and wrist warmers. Lots of things that beginners and more experienced knitters can make. And I'll include intricate patterns for lace weight shawls and patterns for jumpers and cardigans.'

'And bees.'

I nodded. 'Bees are cute. They're attractive.' Not half as attractive as the beemaster. He was standing close to me. I could see how beautiful his blue eyes were. 'And that's just one aspect. There will be sewing patterns and all sorts of crafts as well as regular features.'

'What about advertising? Would I be able to advertise my honey?'

'You could, but I'm only having ads that are craft related or suitable for the magazine, and written as features, as advertorials.'

'So I couldn't buy advertising space in your magazine?'

'It would be written as part of a feature. I could mention your honey, give a link to your products. I'm sure readers would enjoy finding out what a beemaster does. I'd include the editorial near the bumblebee tea cosy. The features would complement each other.'

'How much would that cost me? I've been thinking of advertising again, but I've been so busy I haven't had time to chat to the press. A couple of newspapers and magazines contact me every few months to see if I want to advertise with them, and sometimes I send out a press release.'

I handed him a list of the magazine's advertising rates.

He cast a glance at it. 'This is very reasonable.'

'Obviously the magazine has to build a substantial readership.'

'Yes, but I'm interested. I'd like to be included.'

'Okay. I'll need a couple of high resolution photographs and some editorial. I can do an interview with you, or you can write the equivalent of a press release and I'll mould it to suit the feature. You'll have approval before anything is published.'

'And it's published only online?'

'Yes. I'm planning to create a regular following for the magazine. A strong readership. It'll take a few issues, but I've seen how the right features, interesting patterns and plenty to make and read, can turn a magazine around. I'm going to put everything I know that works into the one magazine.'

'What if I wanted to advertise regularly?'

'There will be standard ads on the magazine's website. I'm planning to have lots of interesting things on the website itself, including videos showing how to knit, how to cut a pattern, papercrafting. Tips, hints and techniques. You could place an ad on the website, or I could add you into another appropriate feature.

15

There will be recipes, especially baking. Maybe you'd like to be part of something like that — honey used for baking a cake.'

He kept nodding as I spoke.

'I'll jot down a few things about my honey and look out some photographs. Drop by anytime and we'll chat.'

'Great.'

He finished his tea and I saw him to the front door. The night sky arched above us, twinkling with stars.

'Thanks for the tea.' He walked away, and then turned and said, 'Have you ever had to use those boxing skills of yours?'

'Sometimes. Mainly when men step out of line,' I said lightly.

'I'll make sure to be on my best behaviour.'

I heard the laughter in his voice as he walked away, becoming a shadow as he headed down the countryside road that led to his cottage.

I closed the door and sighed. A beemaster feature would be interesting, especially if it included a photograph of Bredon. I'd seen the effect a handsome man could have in a knitting magazine on Ethel and Hilda. A picture of the beemaster would be perfect for the first issue, particularly if I could persuade him to give us that sexy smile of his. Then again, such thoughts only ever led to one thing. The thing that I was renowned for — trouble.

Later that night, I checked out Bredon's website after editing new patterns that had been emailed to me from contacts I'd made during the past several months. They were freelance crafters — a papercrafter and someone who loved crochet, and I'd known them from working on the London magazines. They wanted to contribute patterns in exchange for advertising their crafts.

Bredon's website had plenty of information, so I wrote a five hundred word editorial highlighting the things I thought readers would find interesting. I planned to take this with me when I went to interview him. Experience had taught me that regardless of people saying they'd write some notes or a press release and look out photographs to go with the feature, few did this without continued prompting. It was a whole lot easier to turn up with a rough they could read, amend if necessary and approve.

According to Bredon's website, beekeeping had been part of his family's business and he'd gained a love of working with bees since he was a boy. He'd been born and raised in central Scotland, but had

16

moved to the cottage after losing his parents. It stated that he'd always loved the coast and the countryside. During the year he travelled throughout the UK and abroad to attend events and give talks on his work, and to promote his own range of honey which was sold through select outlets.

It mentioned that his bees loved Tavion's fields of flowers and how the taste of each honey harvest varied according to the selection of flowers the bees chose to visit.

There was information about how to create a bee garden by adding flowers that bees loved such as lavender and delphiniums. My mind starting thinking of including this type of information and providing a list of flowers that bees frequented — both honeybees and bumblebees. I could merge this with the floral embroidery patterns. I'd already prepared several flower outlines for embroidery work and these included lavender and delphiniums along with chocolate daisies, cornflowers, teasel and sweet peas. And I'd edited and formatted a sewing pattern to make an old–fashioned pincushion from a scabiosa flower print. Scabiosa were sometimes called pincushion flowers. These were on Bredon's list as a favourite with the bees.

The photographs on his website were excellent and as he'd taken them himself there were no picture credits necessary. He had beautiful shots of honeycombs, jars of honey and some of himself in action installing bees into a new hive. These would give an ideal presentation of the beemaster at work, and they made his honey look golden and delicious. I also wanted to include a picture of Bredon — a handsome shot without the protective head gear. Why not make the most of having a good looking guy in the opening issue. Eye candy, or in his case, honey.

I closed the laptop, and before putting the lights off at around 2:00am, I looked out the window. Bredon's cottage was in darkness. Perhaps he was trying to set a good example. A hint that I should get to sleep at a decent hour.

# CHAPTER THREE

## Patchwork Fairy

Big Sam had a patchwork fairy appliqué on his shirt pocket. He seemed quite happy with it. He nodded to me as I walked across the grass to Ethel's cottage. The front door was open and a number of women were already there, some sipping tea and chatting outside in the sunshine, others inside. It looked busy. Most of them wore summery dresses, similar to the cotton floral print I'd chosen, or cool separates. The afternoon was a scorcher. The warm breeze wafting up from the shore tempted me to abandon everything and enjoy sunbathing on the sand and swimming in the glistening blue–green sea. I didn't yield to temptation. Maybe another day. Today I'd promised to have afternoon tea at Ethel's cottage and chat to the ladies.

A pretty young woman smoothed her hand down the fairy appliqué, patting it as if delighted with it. Had she sewn it on Sam's shirt? I'd tried to find out about the people who lived in the area who were experts at sewing and crafting. I was sure this was Ione. I'd seen her website and thought her fairy dolls were exquisite. Sam smiled at her, leaned down, because he was extremely tall and she was even smaller than me, and whispered something to her that brought a squeal of glee. I assumed they were dating. She seemed enthralled with him.

He acknowledged me with less warmth than the last time we'd met. 'Aurora. How are you these days? Keeping yourself busy with this magazine?'

'Glad to be back at the cottage. Hoping to make a fresh start.' And to leave the past behind. Including the interlude with him.

'All the best with it.' He didn't sound entirely pleased. I mentally scored him off my list of those who welcomed me home. A list of no one actually. Not one, not even Sam.

I sighed inwardly. Never mind. I didn't want to become involved with him again. This was easier. I'd always worked better when starting with a clean slate.

I left him to whisper and flirt with Ione while I stepped inside Ethel's cottage. Some places appear smaller when you've been away for a while, but the cottage was bigger. Then I realised she'd added an extension on to the area where she worked, spinning and dyeing her yarn. A number of women drinking tea and coffee and standing around gossiping and eating cake stopped the moment they saw me, as if someone had cast a spell on them.

Keep your nerve I told myself. If they weren't interested in the magazine they wouldn't be out in force. They wanted to be part of it. I could sense the anticipation. Lots of sewing and knitting projects, finished items, spilled from their craft bags. They'd brought their wares for me to see. Yes, they wanted to be involved in the magazine. They just needed to put me through the mincer before admitting it.

Let the grinding begin.

'We hear you were flashing your knickers at the beemaster,' said Hilda.

Yes, here we go.

'I was stuck. He helped me climb in the front window of my cottage. I'd locked myself out,' I explained.

Another woman chimed–in. 'We heard that Bredon left your cottage late at night.'

'It wasn't that late. We were talking about the magazine. He's interested in advertising his honey and being included in one of the features.'

This news perked them up and they turned their attention to the beemaster.

'What feature is he in?' said Ethel.

'Knit a bee tea cosy. His editorial will be on the double–page spread featuring the knitting pattern.'

'Have you got the pattern for the bee tea cosy?' asked Ethel.

'No. I was hoping one of you would be interested in making it.'

'Judith's the tea cosy knitting expert,' said Ethel.

It was then that I noticed a black cat, Thimble, sitting outside the back window on the ledge peering in. I followed his line of vision and saw Judith. I hadn't recognised her at first because she was now a stunning blonde.

Judith, a woman in her mid–fifties who worked as the dressmaker's assistant, looked over at me. No smile, but at least she was here and her bag was brimming with knitting. She dug out a sparkly turquoise blue tea cosy and handed it to me.

I'm sure they all saw the surprise on my face, not because Judith seemed to have put aside our past differences, but because of the tea cosy.

'This is exactly what I was hoping for,' I said, admiring the lovely ribbed cosy. 'I wanted a sparkly sea blue ribbed cosy as one of the tea cosy patterns.'

'The dressmaker suggested I bring it along,' said Judith. 'I knitted it last night. It's my own pattern, a traditional pattern. The rib stitch is very attractive and makes up into a pretty tea cosy. You can use it for your magazine if you want. I can also give you a bumblebee tea cosy pattern.'

'Thank you, Judith. That would be great.'

Ethel handed me a cup of tea. 'What other knitting patterns are you looking for? And do you want a feature about spinning and dyeing yarn?'

I brought out a bundle of papers from my satchel. 'I printed out copies of the pagination sheets for the magazine.' These were handed around and studied eagerly. 'This is a basic list of all the features I propose for the first issue and the pages each feature will be on. I've already edited and prepared half the content for the magazine from crafter contacts I've worked with before. They want to be part of this new magazine. They're not being paid. Instead, they're using it as a form of advertising. On this other sheet, I've listed details you'll probably want to know such as how much profit I aim to make in the first six issues, advertising costs, for those like Bredon, and eventually how much each of you would be paid for writing features and contributing patterns once the magazine was in profit.'

Ethel handed out the second set of papers. She kept one and studied it herself. 'But what we're really looking at is free advertising for ourselves in your magazine?'

'Yes. If I can whip up enough interest in the magazine, I'll make a profit from the sales of it rather than from standard advertising. I'm hoping this will give the magazine a strong readership. Each issue will be packed with lots of patterns and plenty to read without masses of ads.'

Ione spoke up. 'How much will it cost people to buy your online magazine?'

'About half the price of an average print magazine.'

The women nodded, taking all this in.

'Could I have one of my fairy doll patterns, a sewing pattern, in the magazine?' Ione asked.

'Yes. I've listed a doll feature on the pagination sheet. A rag doll or fairy type doll to sew.'

'How do we go about this?' Ethel asked.

'I thought we'd chat about the items I already have and those I'd like to include and see if any of you have things that are suitable.'

Ethel bustled off to the kitchen sounding enthusiastic. 'I'll get you a slice of chocolate cake, Aurora. You used to like it. I baked one specially for you.'

'Thanks, Ethel. That would be lovely.'

And so we had tea, cake and chatted about the magazine, and I was introduced to Mairead, Tiree and several others who were new to the area. I also met Hilda's sister, Jessie, who had come over from one of the islands for the afternoon meeting. They were alike in their craft interests, both being quilters, but I was particularly keen on Jessie's cross stitch and embroidery patterns. Jessie offered to give me templates for floral embroidery and gold work along with a cross stitch pattern.

'Is anyone into papercraft?' I said. 'This is very popular.'

'I love my papercraft,' said one of the women.

'Me two,' said another.

'I'm interested in various types of papercraft,' I said. 'For the first issue I'm looking for vintage scraps and scrapbooking projects.'

'Vintage scraps?' said Hilda. 'You mean those paper scraps with flowers or pretty figures, like fairies, on them. We used to have them at school when I was a girl. We tucked them into the pages of a paperback book and exchanged them with each other. I haven't seen scraps for years.'

'Yes, that's them,' I said. 'I want to have a couple of A4 sheets of scraps that readers can print out. They need to be our designs. So if anyone is inclined to do some artwork...'

A few of them looked at Mairead. 'I'd be happy to draw and paint them.'

'Mairead's a botanical illustrator,' said Ethel. 'She painted that picture of my cottage. It's beautiful.' Ethel pointed to the painting on the wall.

'It really is beautiful,' I said.

21

'What type of artwork do you want for the scraps?' Mairead asked.

'Flowers, baskets of flowers, anything vintage, perhaps items for afternoon tea — a floral teapot, cups, cakes.'

Mairead nodded. 'I'll sketch some roughs and let you see them before I paint them.'

'And I'd like any illustrative pen and ink drawings suitable for adult colouring in,' I said. 'Each magazine will have four pages of artwork to colour in with pens or coloured pencils. These will be printable from the website.'

'All my botanical drawings start as pencil sketches,' said Mairead. 'Then I illustrate further with pen and ink or paint them as watercolours. I could let you have some pen and ink florals and other designs if you like.'

'Perfect. Thanks, Mairead.'

The two other women who were into scrapbooking agreed to team up to create a vintage scrapbook using stamping, lace, fabric and ribbon that readers could make.

One of the ladies made and sold her jewellery online. 'I have a beautiful pearl bracelet design and a diamante brooch. I've also got a wedding tiara design made from wire and crystals, and satin bridal slippers that you stitch with sequins and sparkle.'

'I'll put these in the bridal feature,' I said.

Ethel smiled. 'We're all looking forward to the weddings coming up, aren't we girls?' She referred to Mairead and Tiree.

'It's early days,' said Tiree, blushing slightly. 'Tavion hasn't actually proposed.'

Mairead kept quiet.

Ethel grinned at Tiree. 'I've heard that Tavion has asked you to move out of your cottage and into his house.'

Ione's eyes sparkled. 'Has he? How romantic. Are you going to move in with him soon?'

Tiree blushed even more. 'I've been thinking about it.'

'The dressmaker thinks she should,' Judith told us.

'Oh, we're going to have to help plan the wedding,' said Ethel. 'I love weddings, just as long as I'm not the one getting a band of gold on my finger. Those days are past for me.'

Judith frowned at her. 'The postmaster will be disappointed to hear that.'

Ethel swept her comment aside. 'Ach, he's an old scallywag. I like things the way they are between us. I run and he chases me.'

'Does he ever catch you?' I asked Ethel.

'Nope. Not yet, though I came close recently and had to hide in Tiree's garden. I'm not as fast as I used to be. Then again, neither is he.'

The ladies laughed. Mairead remained quiet, smiling but giving no hint of when she'd marry Fintry the flower hunter.

Ethel prompted her. 'What about you Mairead? That's a sparkler of a diamond ring Fintry gave you.'

Mairead smiled gently and admired the ring. She explained that he'd recently proposed and presented her with a diamond and white gold engagement ring. 'It is. We haven't set a date yet.'

'Maybe you'll get married in the winter,' said Jessie. 'I was a snow bride and it felt really magical. Even my husband's fishing boat was encrusted with ice that day.' She checked the time. 'Speaking of which, I promised him I'd be back at the harbour by now. He'll be waiting for me. We're sailing back across to the island, so I'll see you all another time.' She looked at me. 'I'll keep this sheet of paper and speak to you about the patterns soon. I'll start looking through my quilts and designs this evening when I get home.'

We waved Jessie off and continued making plans.

Bit by bit the magazine was coming together.

'I'm happy to photograph any of the projects,' I said. 'And we're in a unique position to use the lovely environment and the cottages as backgrounds for the photographs. In London, we had to set up things like this.' I pointed to Ethel's table, covered with an embroidered linen tablecloth and set with two cake stands. Everything from the teacups to the old–fashioned teapot and wholesome home baking, created a perfect photo–shoot scene. 'I think most of you have been taking photographs for the items you sell on your websites and other online shops.'

'I use a camera and photograph my quilts outdoors to show the colours,' said Hilda. 'I hang them over the washing line or from tree branches.'

'I take pictures of my fairies with my phone,' said Ione, which prompted a number of the women to agree that their phones gave them great pictures.

'Well,' I said. 'I can crop and adjust any of the photographs if necessary. Please remember to avoid any brand name products in the pictures. We can't use those. Focus only on your work and the setting. If you're not confident to take the pictures of your knitting or sewing or whatever you've made, tell me and I'll help with that.'

'I'll help too,' said Judith. 'I enjoy taking photographs.'

'Great,' I said. 'I'm sure if we all pull together we can create something wonderful with this magazine. Lots of patterns, lovely photographs, plenty of hints and tips. Remember, all the patterns and designs have to be your own, they have to belong to you and be original. Once you have your pattern finished, email it to me. I've put my email on the pagination sheets and my phone number. Email the editorial and the photographs. Or you can write it out and hand it in to me.'

'This is so exciting,' said Tiree. 'I haven't had a chance to think about what I'd like to make.' She glanced at the sheet. 'I love quilting, sewing obviously being the dressmaker's apprentice. Recently, she's been teaching me how to make vintage–style collars. I've designed my own templates and they sew up lovely into collars that you can add to a plain neck dress or top. Would these be useful?'

'They definitely would, Tiree.'

She smiled. 'I'll email the collar patterns to you tonight and some pictures of what I've made from them. Some are made from floral print fabrics and others have sequins added and are almost like necklaces with plenty of sparkle. And you're welcome to come along to the sewing bee at my cottage tomorrow night. I live in the old strawberry jam cottage down near the harbour.'

'I know it. I'll be there.'

Ethel agreed to include a lace weight shawl pattern she'd designed, and give tips on spinning yarn. She read the pagination sheet and asked about the regular features I'd listed at the end. 'What are these?'

'Regular features will include a recipe page,' I said. 'Probably a cake or sweet recipe. That chocolate cake of yours would be tasty if it's your own concoction.'

'The chocolate sponge cake certainly is,' said Ethel. 'The silky smooth chocolate ganache is the chocolatier's recipe. I asked Jaec

Midwinter how he made his cakes so delicious and he told me. It makes the cake taste as rich and chocolaty as fudge.'

'We would need to ask his permission to use his recipe,' I said.

'I'll talk to him,' said Ethel. 'It's a pity we didn't take a picture of the cake before we ate it. There's nothing left except crumbs. I'll bake another one.'

'I'll come over and help you test the quality,' Mairead joked with her.

'Me too,' said Hilda.

'Another regular feature will be quilt block designs,' I said. 'Ideally, I'd like three quilt blocks per issue.'

'I can handle that for you,' said Hilda.

Tiree nodded. 'I'll help with those as well.'

'And the colouring in pages,' I said. 'These can be printed out and coloured in or used as embroidery patterns. Luckily, we'll have Mairead's botanical illustrations and artwork for those.'

Mairead smiled and nodded.

'I've also been offered a romance series,' I told them. 'I haven't accepted it yet. I wanted to see what you thought. I like the idea of having a romance in the magazine. I know it's a craft magazine, but I've read the story and it's entertaining. And it has a craft theme.'

The idea was given a huge thumbs up by the ladies. I hadn't expected them to be so keen.

'I love a bit of romance,' said Ethel. 'It reminds me of the magazines I used to read many years ago. I enjoyed them.'

'I'm trying to turn the clock back to the magazines of the past, regarding the type of content, while forging ahead to the future by making it available in the digital age. The best of both worlds. That's what's at the core of my plan. I think it should work. I already implemented many of these ideas in London and they were very successful.'

'A romance story in the magazine would be brilliant,' Hilda agreed.

I smiled. 'I'll contact the author and let her know she'll be part of the magazine.'

For the next two hours we discussed patterns and projects until it was time to start heading home for dinner. The atmosphere was enthusiastic and I imagined all the busy hands that would be working on their crafts later that night — sewing dolls, designing quilt blocks, scrapbooking, sketching, dressmaking, knitting, felting, tapestry, embroidery, crochet and jewellery making. We were all going to be busy.

Judith made an announcement before everyone left. 'The dressmaker has offered to give you one of her dress patterns.'

'Really?' I said. 'A designer dress pattern from the dressmaker would certainly be popular. Tell her yes, and thank you.'

'It'll need to be enlarged, piece by piece, when readers print it out,' Judith explained. 'But most people are used to doing this for dress pattern printouts.'

'Yes, of course,' I said. My mind was already thinking that this could be a newsworthy inclusion. The dressmaker's designs weren't available. This would be something really special.'

# CHAPTER FOUR

## The Beemaster's Cottage

I drove back to my cottage and noticed Bredon was in his garden working at the beehives. I checked the time. Dinner time. I parked the car and wondered what to do. Should I show him the editorial I'd written? I decided no. I didn't want to intrude at this time in case he thought I was angling for dinner with him.

I was about to drive on, but he saw me and waved me over. I considered pretending not to notice, but it was obvious I'd seen him, so I drove over and parked in the narrow lane outside his front garden.

I got out as he came striding over to me, smiling, pleased to see me. That's the impression I got and my stomach tightened nervously.

'I was going to stop for dinner. Would you like to join me?' he said, looking like he'd spent the afternoon in the sun, all burnished and hot gold. His eyes were particularly sparkly and it was hard to refuse such a warm invitation.

'I've just finished chatting to the women about the magazine at Ethel's cottage. I was heading home. I don't want you to feel obliged to invite me to dinner.'

'I'd welcome the company. Come on, you can lend me a hand if you like. It's nothing fancy.'

I followed him inside his cottage. I liked the atmosphere. Unlike my cottage perched on the hillside, the beemaster's cottage felt grounded, wrapped in warm sunshine, buzzing with happy bees and lush with the scent of the garden flowers. There was something old–fashioned about his cottage even though the interior was warm honey shades from palest lemon to chestnut and bronze. A manly house and yet so picturesque.

'The kitchen's through here.' He stood in the doorway looking at the silly woman staring wide–eyed and rather envious of his lovely house.

'Sorry. I was just admiring the cottage.'

'You like it?'

'I do. I still don't feel at home in mine yet.'

'Give yourself time. And without wanting to seem like I'm nagging you, you really do need to cut back on all the hours you're working.'

I smiled and headed into the kitchen. He started washing his hands before searching the fridge for whatever he planned to cook.

'What?' he said, glancing round at me.

'I thought you'd notice the lights on in my cottage late last night.'

'Very late.'

'You must've been up too if you were watching.'

He brought a selection of salad vegetables from the fridge and put them on the table. 'No, I was in bed. My window has a view across the fields and there's this little cottage that's a beacon of light and activity every evening. Sometimes I want to use a flashlight and signal to her — get some sleep. You work too hard.'

'I have to work hard.'

'I know.'

We gazed at each other for a moment and then he turned the hob on and began to cook breaded fish for us. 'I hope fish and salad will suffice.'

'Yes, that would be lovely.' I set about preparing the salad and we chatted while we worked. It gave me the strangest feeling, nervous and yet comfortable.

He told me about installing new bees in one of the hives, how the bees are put inside the hive and then the queen added.

'She's kept inside a private casing to settle in. The other bees need time to accept her as their queen. I sometimes think of it as dating. If I'm attracted to a woman I'll take my time getting to know her, letting her know me.'

I blushed as bright as the crisp red peppers in the salad. I couldn't look at him and concentrated on my meal. 'And has this method worked for you?'

He spread his arms out and laughed. 'Apparently not. I live here alone and haven't dated anyone in over a year. To be fair, I've been extremely busy with work and travelling up and down to London and attending conferences abroad.'

'It sounds as if you work too hard.'

He laughed again. 'I do. So where does that leave us?'

'Us?'

'Forgive me. I'm a complete idiot when it comes to chatting to beautiful women.'

I continued to blush, and took a sip of my iced mineral water.

'I don't mean to embarrass you.'

'I'm eh...flattered, but I'm at odds and unsettled with everything in my life right now. And you're...well...you're...'

Those fabulous blue eyes of his pulled me in. 'I'm what?'

Another sip of mineral. The warmth of my hands was melting the ice in the glass. 'You're...' What? Totally gorgeous. Sexy. Handsome and charming. Someone save me from melting and giving in to all the feelings erupting inside me. I should've been at home, dining alone, instead of cooking dinner with this handsome man and then having to face him across the table and discuss how luscious he was.

'I'm what?'

'A talking point with the ladies.' The editor in me sifted out the other words such as sexy and hot as hell.

He grinned, and the dimples in his cheeks made my heart squeeze.

'I thought Fintry, the flower hunter, was the main focus of their attention.'

I shook my head. 'He's asked Mairead to marry him. The ring on her finger is a dazzler.'

'Jaec Midwinter, then.'

'I haven't met the chocolatier, so I'll reserve my judgement.'

He smiled and we continued joking with each other.

'Tavion.'

I shook my head again. 'Nope. He's asked Tiree to move in with him.'

A flash of blue. 'Has he?'

I smiled. 'You're worse than the ladies for enjoying gossip.'

'No one is worse than the ladies round here. Okay, what about Big Sam?'

'He's involved with Ione. She's sewn a fairy appliqué on his shirt.'

'That's him claimed then, eh?'

I shrugged. 'Ione did have a crush on you. Ethel told me.'

'Ione's a nice girl but there's no attraction on my part.'

'That just leaves you and the postmaster.'

'Do you think Ethel will ever let him catch her?' he said.

'He did in the past.'

'Did he?'

'Yes, so that's more gossip for you.'

'If it's true about Judith and the harbour master, I'm throwing in the towel right now.'

'Judith's involved with the harbour master?' I said.

'No, I'm just making things up. That's what folk do round here, isn't it?'

'It is.'

'Hopefully no one will find out about us having dinner.'

I took a sip of water. 'That's the last thing we need.' I almost let slip about them haranguing me for flashing my knickers at him. Thankfully, I buttoned my lips.

There was a knock at the front door, or rather the buzz of the doorbell. His bell sounded like a buzzing bee. I tried not to laugh.

Bredon went to see who it was and then came hurrying back through to the kitchen. 'It's Judith.'

'What does she want?'

'I have no idea, but I'll have to invite her in, so unless you want the gossipmongers to have a field day, I'd hide if I were you.'

He went back through to let her in.

I panicked, which was ridiculous, but Bredon was right. Knicker flashing, Bredon leaving my cottage late at night, and then having dinner with him all cosy in his kitchen. The gossip would be awful. I took his advice, but where to hide? I heard Judith's voice and made a dash for the back door, but it was locked. The kitchen window was open. In hindsight, I should have opted to hide in the laundry cupboard.

The window was open quite wide and I made an attempt to shimmy through it. Unfortunately, the hem of my dress snagged on the ledge and I tumbled. Stuck halfway, I struggled to free myself as Judith walked into the kitchen chatting to Bredon about knitting a bee tea cosy.

Judith gasped. 'Why is Aurora trying to climb inside your kitchen window?'

Bredon remained calm, on the surface, and came over to help me. 'I think she's trying to climb outside rather than in.'

Accusing eyes raked over the remnants of our meal. 'I'm sorry I interrupted your...whatever you two were up to.'

'We were having dinner,' Bredon said, helping me climb back in, and lifting me with ease inside. He put me down and I straightened my dress.

'We were discussing his editorial for the magazine.' Not that I owed Judith an explanation.

Bredon opened a cupboard and selected two jars of honey for Judith. 'These would look good in your photographs. This one is a set honey and the other is clear amber.' He handed them to her.

She clasped them and looked delighted. 'I want to put them beside my bee tea cosy for the magazine photographs. It was the dressmaker's idea to ask you for the honey. I thought I'd pop in on my way home. I'll give you the honey back when I've finished taking the pictures.'

'No, keep the honey, Judith,' he said.

'I'll bake you a honey cake,' she told him.

He smiled at her. 'Sounds delicious.'

'Perhaps you could include the cake in the photographs?' I suggested.

'Yes, I'm trying to think what would look appropriate to go with the bee theme of the feature. Most of my table covers and other things in my kitchen are blue and pink.' She looked around Bredon's kitchen. 'Yours looks like it belongs to a beemaster — sunshine yellow, pale lemon and amber colours. And I love your wee nick–nacks.' She pointed to the beehive biscuit jar and bee salt and pepper dishes.

We probably had the same thought at the same time. Bredon's kitchen would be perfect for a photo–shoot for the bee tea cosy.

'You're welcome to take the photographs here, Judith, if it's better for you,' he said. He opened the laundry cupboard. 'People tend to give me gifts with bees on them, and someone gave me a yellow table cover. Yes, here it is.' He held it up. Bees and hives were printed on the fabric.

Judith nodded and looked at me. 'What do you think, Aurora.'

'It would be a great background for the photos. This is the type of set up we'd have to arrange specially in a studio when I worked in London, but here with all these beautiful cottages and lovely scenery it's already perfect.'

'That's settled then,' said Bredon.

Judith was delighted with this idea, and as he showed her out I sat down at the kitchen table and sighed. Extra fuel had been given to the gossipmongers.

Bredon came back through. 'More tea?'

I stood up. 'I should go. People are going to start gossiping about us.'

'I think that boat has already sailed, don't you?'

I sat back down, and he started to make us another pot of tea.

'It's getting hot in here,' he said.

Oh yes indeedy. I kept looking at him, admiring the way the muscles on his forearms rippled and tensed as he poured the boiling water, and how he moved around the kitchen. Every woman should have a Bredon in their kitchen I thought. Perpetual entertainment and luscious eye candy. I'd never get a shred of work done, but my goodness, I'd be happy.

He picked up the teapot and put it on a tray along with our cups. 'Let's sit outside in the front garden. I can bore you with my knowledge of bees and hives while we have a relaxing cuppa.'

I followed him out and we sat at a wooden table amid his beautiful flower–filled garden with its beehives old and new.

'Some of the hives are very old–fashioned. I like the vintage style, and the bees adore them, so I try to keep them in good condition. Others are new, like the one over there. I've just installed hundreds of bees in that hive today. They're settling nicely.' He cupped his hand to his ear. 'You can here the low buzz of them, especially on evenings like this when the air is warm and clear.'

He continued to tell me about his bees, and I listened to him and to the bees whose sound was strangely comforting. I felt myself relax, really relax.

Then a tractor rolled by in the distance along one of the fields bordering Bredon's property. The farmer waved to us. Bredon waved back.

I tensed. 'More gossip.'

'I feel like the lesser spotted beemaster,' he said calmly. 'Oh look, there he is having tea and crumpet with that troublemaker Aurora.'

I started to laugh.

'She's flashed her knickers at him twice now —'

I cut–in. 'You heard about that?'

'Hasn't everyone?'

'It's not twice,' I corrected him. 'Only once.'

He grinned.

My mind rewound to the recent climbing out the window incident. Surely not. 'You didn't see my...'

He nodded. 'Judith probably did too. It was the way you were contorted trying to scramble out the window. Just for the record — I quite like thongs.'

'I'm not wearing a thong,' I shouted. 'My knickers got a bit twisted, that's all.'

Bredon smiled in sheer amusement. '*Aurora gets her knickers in a twist in beemaster's cottage.* Maybe the postmaster will put it on his notice board.'

I tensed even more. Judith was sure to tell everyone. 'It looked bad, didn't it?'

'Yep.'

'There is no real privacy living here,' I complained.

'Not for a trouble magnet and a man like me. We're ripe for gossip fodder. I bet that even if we were holed up in my bedroom, someone would come knocking at the window and catch us.'

By now I was wide–eyed. My mind had cherry–picked the choicest words — *holed up in his bedroom.*

He realised his gaff. 'Not that I'm hinting about having you in my bedroom.'

I glared even more.

'You know what I mean, Aurora.'

'Yes. My trouble magnet vibe extends to you when we're in the same vicinity. I should keep well out of your way.'

'Nonsense. You know the best way to diffuse smatterings of silly gossip?'

Did this man know something that even the gossip columns in the press didn't know? I listened carefully.

'Give them a whopper to chew on.'

I gasped. I did.

For the first time that evening, I saw Bredon blush. 'Sorry, I'd didn't mean what you think. I meant — when Judith, Ethel and the others are gossiping about silly stuff, tell them a big ridiculous lie and they'll talk about that and then the trivial gossip will fizzle out.'

'What about the big slice of gossip? Won't that make things worse?'

'No, it'll burn bright and then fade as they realise how silly they are.'

I wasn't sure about Bredon's gossip–control technique.

He was confident it would work. 'I've done things like this before. Of course, not with the ultimate troublemaker like yourself, but it's bound to work, sort of.'

'What would you tell them about us?' I couldn't imagine what it would be.

He shrugged and seemed to make something up on the spot. 'I'll tell them I'm going to ask you to marry me before the end of the summer. That'll keep them busy.'

I was momentarily stunned. 'That really is a big fat lie.' Wasn't it?

The look he gave me insinuated I'd insulted him. 'Does it sound so awful that I'd propose marriage to you?'

'Eh no, I mean yes, erm...yes, no, what?'

He laughed. 'That's the best answer a woman has given me in years.'

A car pulled up at the garden gate. Tavion got out. He smiled and approached us.

'Let's try it out on Tavion for effect. Let's see his reaction to our engagement news.'

'No, Bredon, no,' I yelled at him. But it was too late.

'I hope I'm not interrupting anything special,' said Tavion. He was a very attractive man with dark hair and hazel eyes.

'Actually, I've just asked Aurora to marry me.'

'No,' I shouted.

Tavion glanced at Bredon and gave him a man–to–man look, then he mumbled, 'Sorry she's turned you down, Bredon. I'm sorry.' Without letting either of us explain, Tavion jumped into his car and drove off.

'We'll see how that flies.' I heard the bravado in Bredon's voice.

'I don't think that went according to plan, did it?'

He put his hands on his lean hips and sighed. 'Bloomin' gossipmongers.'

# CHAPTER FIVE

## Botanical Art Designs

The next morning I had an email from Judith with the subject heading — do you have an engagement gift list?

My stomach churned so much I couldn't face making breakfast.

Mairead phoned. 'Is it true?'

'No, it's not. Bredon was being farcical. It was a silly joke that backfired.'

'I have several pieces of artwork that could be suitable for the magazine. I was going to invite you down to see them, then I heard about the proposal when I was in the shops this morning and thought I should call you. Do you want to come down and chat or hide?'

I smiled. 'I'd like that.' Especially the hiding part.

'Fintry is away sailing up and down the Firth of Forth this morning, testing out the new sails and rigging on his yacht,' said Mairead. 'He won't be back until later. Come down for a cuppa and some girl talk.'

'Thanks, I'm on my way.'

Mairead lived with Fintry in the flower hunter's cottage. The garden was one of the most beautiful I'd ever seen, filled with flowers from all over the world.

'I've put the kettle on,' Mairead said, welcoming me in. Her copper brown hair was tied back in a loose ponytail and she looked fresh–faced and happy. She wore a blue cotton shift dress that emphasised her bright blue eyes. 'I'm working on my botanical art for my publishers in London. The book includes floral design motifs for quilting and embroidery. I had a look through my designs and found plenty of extra floral pieces I thought you might like for the magazine. And teacup, cakes and afternoon tea designs for the vintage scraps. I've put them on the table. Have a look while I make the tea.'

Her artwork table was at the window in the living room. The window was open and the scent of the flowers wafted in on the sea breeze. The pen and ink drawings were magnificent. 'These are fantastic, Mairead. They'd be great for the colouring in sheets that readers will download from the website. And they're ideal for embroidery and appliqué templates — and as vintage scraps.'

Mairead brought the tea and biscuits through. 'I'm pleased you like them. There is a mix of flowers — candytuft 'needlepoint' which I designed for embroidery, sunflowers, tea roses, old–fashioned four o'clocks, delphiniums, heliotrope, fuchsia, snapdragons, sea holly, thistles and pansies. And I included some dragons, sea dragons and seahorse designs.'

I wanted all of them. Every single design. 'They're all so beautiful. I'm not sure which ones to choose. Definitely the candytuft and the four o'clocks which are perfect for vintage items, and the delphiniums —'

'You're welcome to use them all. Even if you only use a few in each issue.'

'Oh that would be brilliant, thank you, Mairead. I'll include editorial about you and your artwork in the features.' I gazed at the drawings and designs, picturing how these would fit into the format. I also noticed that she had her sewing machine set up and had been quilting.

'It's great living here,' she said. 'No wonder you decided to move back.'

'London wasn't for me. Even though I'm not settled yet, I feel this is where I belong.'

'When I came here in January, I never imagined I'd be engaged by the summer, especially to the flower hunter whose cottage I'd rented. I didn't know he'd be so handsome and exciting.' She cupped her tea and gazed out at the sea. In the distance was a white yacht with blue and white sails. Fintry's yacht. 'I hope you find the type of happiness here that I have.' She paused. 'What about you and Bredon? I don't really know him, but I feel as though I do with all the talk from Ethel and the others. And I've seen him.'

'He's a looker, that's for sure.'

'Do you think there was maybe more to it when he joked about marrying you?'

I shook my head. 'We've only just met.'

'The first time I met Fintry I thought — wow! I didn't know who he was. And now look.' She held up her hand to show me the diamond sparkler on her finger. Then she went over to the sewing machine where she had a stash of fabric. 'The dressmaker gave me a gift. She gave me all this oyster silk fabric. She's hand sewn metallic silver and gold thread on some of it.'

'It's beautiful.'

Mairead ran her hands across the fabric. 'They say that the dressmaker sews magic into the fabric. She wrote me a note saying I'd know what to do with the fabric when the time came.'

'And do you?'

'Yes, I'm going to make it into my wedding dress. Once we set a date.' She folded the fabric and tucked it away carefully. 'I don't want to sew a stitch though until we've actually agreed on a date for the wedding. Maybe I'll be a snow bride after all. I've always loved the winter, the snow. The cottage was covered in snow when I moved here. It felt quite magical, and that would be nice.' She smiled. 'So what are we going to do about all this gossip with you and the beemaster? Would you like me to tell Ethel and the others what happened?'

'Would you mind? I always seem to be making excuses.'

'It's the sewing bee tonight at Tiree's cottage. Come with me and we'll sort out the gossip.'

Through the window we saw Fintry's yacht sailing home towards the harbour. I got up to leave, taking Mairead's artwork with me.

Mairead shaded her eyes with her hand, causing her floral cluster ring to sparkle like white fire in the sunlight as she looked towards Fintry's yacht.

'Franklin, my publisher, has arranged for some people to come up to the cottage tomorrow to film Fintry and his flower hunter garden while the weather is like this. Our books won't be published for months, but Franklin wants to capture photographs of the garden looking its best. And that's why Fintry has put new sails on his yacht. They're going to take photos of him on the deck and sailing along the coast.'

'The garden is certainly looking fantastic.'

Mairead smiled at me. 'Franklin's planning on using the footage and pictures to start marketing the books, releasing information to the media. He thinks they'll pick up on Fintry's flower hunting especially when the garden is filled with flowers. According to Ethel, this is the warmest summer in years. It's supposed to last until September, but as there's no guarantee, all the filming and pictures are being shot tomorrow. Drop by if you want to see the pandemonium. They'll be here all day and into the evening. They want some night shots of the moon garden aspect. The flowers that are white or open their petals at night.'

'I'll do that. I'm interested in having a peek.'

'I'm sure Ethel and everyone else will too.' Then she stifled a wicked grin. 'Franklin's also asked me to persuade Fintry to take his shirt off for some of the photographs.'

'Gratuitous eye candy. That'll catch the media's attention. If you can get Fintry to whip his shirt off.'

'The thing is, he does that all the time when he's working in the garden. Fintry's not the only man around here who does it.' She gave me a knowing look.

'Bredon.'

'Yes. They've got the physiques for it.' Mairead shrugged. 'If the men have got it, why not flaunt it?'

'Why not indeed. I'll definitely be here. I'll pop down in the morning or the afternoon, or both.'

Mairead laughed. 'Steady on there. Don't get me feeling jealous. I've heard the gossip about you cavorting with Fintry and all the skinny dipping that went on.'

'It wasn't true.' I started to explain and then stopped. Mairead was laughing and clearly winding me up.

She grinned at me. 'So let's sort out this gossip about you marrying the beemaster and your scandalous knicker flashing behaviour tonight at the sewing bee.'

Tiree lived in the former strawberry jam cottage. I made my way there and met Mairead, as arranged, outside it. We'd deliberately arrived fifteen minutes late so that the sewing bee members would be settled.

We stood outside the front door which was open, as were the windows. It was a lovely summer evening and we could hear all the chatter inside. I heard my name mentioned and we eavesdropped on what was said.

'Are you upset that Bredon's asked Aurora to marry him?' said Judith. 'After all, Ione, you fancied him for a while.'

'I'm not as upset as I thought I would be,' said Ione. 'I did have a crush on him, but I'm happy with Big Sam. Though maybe when I see Bredon all toshed up walking down the aisle with Aurora, I might feel a pang of longing for what might have been.'

'I wonder what Aurora's dress will be like?' said Ethel.

'I'm sure the dressmaker will offer her fabric, if she wants,' said Judith. 'She gave Mairead beautiful silk fabric.'

'I'll happily help them sew their wedding dresses,' Tiree added.

'It's good that you're not upset, Ione,' said Ethel, encouraging her to talk about Sam.

I heard the excitement in Ione's voice. 'I love how Sam lifts me up and twirls me around his head like one of my wee fairy dolls. When he does it, I don't have a care in the world. It's just us, giggling and having fun.'

'Sam seems easy to get along with,' said Hilda.

'He is,' Ione agreed. 'I wasted his silver work the other day. I thought all the wee bits of shiny filings on his table were silver paper off a biscuit and brushed them away.'

The women gasped, thinking Sam would've been angry.

Ione continued, 'And do you know what he said to me? He said, "Don't fret, Ione. It's not worth upsetting yourself. You meant well. I'll make some more. It'll be fine." And it was. He made more while I cooked dinner. It was all forgotten. I like that about Sam. No offence to Mairead, but Fintry is too intense for my liking. And no offence to you either, Tiree. Tavion's a bit of a hot head, jumping to the wrong conclusions about a lot of things and then going in a huff with folk. No, I did fancy Bredon, but he's one of those men who is better to be admired. The reality would be exhausting. I'd feel I'd have to be on my best behaviour. And I couldn't see him helping cut out the patterns for my fairies.'

'Sam helps you do that?' said Hilda.

'He does,' said Ione. 'With all his silversmith work, his fingers are so supple, and he can get into all the wee bits for me.'

Ethel snorted.

'Don't you be bad, Ethel,' Ione told her. 'You know fine what I mean. You're as bad as Tavion.'

They all started to laugh.

Mairead gave me a nudge. 'Wait here. I'll go in and tell them about Bredon being silly.'

I waited outside while Mairead put things straight.

I listened to their reaction as Mairead broke the news. I gazed out at the sea, watching the sun sparkle across the surface. The sky stretched for miles without a cloud and it was so hot that even wearing my cotton top and skirt I felt overdressed. Impulsive thoughts dashed through my mind. I could run down to the shore, kick my shoes off and swim in the sea — and to pot with all the gossipmongering.

Mairead popped her head outside the cottage door. 'You can come in now, Aurora.'

I glanced longingly at the sea and then went inside. All the ladies from the afternoon tea meeting were there including Hilda's sister, Jessie.

'So, you're not getting married to the beemaster?' Daggers of accusation were sharp on Hilda's tongue.

'No, I'm not, as Mairead has explained.'

'The dressmaker will be very disappointed,' Judith said to me. 'She loves being involved in weddings, making wedding dresses.'

'Does the dressmaker know about the engagement mistake?' I asked her.

Judith gave me an intense stare. 'The dressmaker knows everything.'

I thought about this while the tea was made, cake cut and Ethel's special tin of shortbread cracked open.

I took a piece of shortbread and balanced it on my saucer while I stirred my tea. As everyone busied around I said, 'If the dressmaker knows everything, she was the one who suggested you go to Bredon's cottage to ask for the jars of honey, Judith.'

My remark hit home. Judith's eyes widened. 'She did. She even insisted it was better to go to his cottage that night on my way home. I had said I'd go in the morning.' She looked thoughtful. 'The dressmaker was so insistent, but why?'

'Maybe the marriage proposal isn't off the agenda after all?' Ethel suggested. 'Perhaps she wanted Judith to catch Bredon and Aurora together.'

Everyone was quiet for a moment, considering this.

'I'll ask her,' Judith said firmly. Her phone rang, interrupting our conversation. 'Yes, okay. I will. I'll tell her.' Judith took a deep breath and said to me, 'That was the dressmaker. She's invited you to have afternoon tea with her tomorrow.'

Some of the ladies gasped. An invitation to go to the dressmaker's cottage was rare. She preferred to limit visitors.

The invitation from the dressmaker wasn't to be taken lightly. 'Tell her thank you. I'll be there tomorrow.'

Judith nodded. 'Two–thirty.'

Tiree offered everyone more tea. She wore her blonde hair pinned up in a messy bun and I loved the dress she wore made from a tea cup printed fabric. Tiree was an extremely pretty young woman. No wonder Tavion had fallen for her. If the gossip about her was true, perhaps this pink cottage would become vacant and we'd have the sewing bee at Tavion's house.

Tiree made me feel welcome and told me to have a look around at any of the fabrics, patterns and items she'd made. While she busied herself in the kitchen, helped by two other ladies making tea, I admired the skirts and tea dresses that were hanging on a rail beside the sewing machines.

'These are gorgeous, Tiree. Did you design them?'

'Yes, though the dressmaker advised me on how to design a traditional tea dress. I've learned a lot of handy techniques as her apprentice.'

'I got your email with the collar pattern templates,' I said. 'The photographs are fantastic. I'd like to include the floral print collar in the first issue, and one of the sequin collar designs in the following issue.'

We chatted about her designs, and then Mairead joined us. 'Did someone mention that there was iced lemonade?'

'Yes,' said Tiree. 'Help yourself. It's in the fridge. Add a scoop of ice cream from the freezer if you want.'

Mairead started to make an ice cream drink while I held up one of Tiree's gorgeous chiffon dresses, wondering if it would fit me and if it was for sale. The three of us were similar in build and age, and I felt comfortable in their company.

'I meant to tell you,' Mairead said to me. 'Franklin's interested in advertising in your magazine. He phoned me to discuss the filming, and I told him about giving you some floral artwork. He thinks the magazine and the book have the same readership — those who are interested in crafts, and he asked me to tell you he'd like to be part of one of the features.'

'Yes,' I said. 'That would be brilliant.'

'I'll give him your contact details and he'll be in touch,' said Mairead.

Tiree asked Mairead about the filming and the other women joined in the conversation.

'Are we allowed to watch?' said Hilda.

'Yes, but the film crew want to focus on Fintry working in his garden, so make sure not to poke your head into the shots.'

'It's quite exciting,' said Ethel. 'This wee community has become a hot bed of publicity and creativity.'

'I never thought I'd be part of a magazine,' Hilda admitted.

'Nor me,' Jessie agreed. 'I'll have the embroidery and cross stitch designs ready for you soon. My husband's been telling the other fishermen that his wife's going to be in a new magazine. He's really chuffed.'

'I've chosen a couple of quilt blocks you can use,' said Hilda. 'I'm also making a quilt block pattern specially for the magazine.'

A few of the bee ladies were already working on items for the first issue, and I noticed that most of them had their pagination sheets with them. Copies had been made and handed round to other members who hadn't been at our initial chat at Ethel's cottage. Word was getting around fast.

'I hope people buy the magazine after all the work that's being put in,' said Ione. 'How are you going to let people know about it?' she asked me.

'I've been developing a presence for it on social media this past year,' I explained. 'I have a lot of subscribers already. I put a newsletter out every couple of weeks with updates on the contents and use any feedback to develop the features. I'm hoping that word of mouth will work. And I'm using the website to give free downloads of patterns and promote it on social media.' I glanced at Judith. 'Having something extra special, such as a pattern from the dressmaker, will certainly be of interest to potential readers and could get us some coverage in the press.'

Judith nodded. 'I've seen the pattern for the dress. It's beautiful. A classic wrapover tea dress that will fit most figures comfortably, though she is including three different size ranges.'

'That's really very generous of her,' I said to Judith. 'It'll be great to launch with that — and all the other things everyone's making.'

# CHAPTER SIX

## The Sewing Bee

At the end of the evening, Fintry came to walk Mairead home.

'Come in, Fintry,' said Tiree. 'Hilda's just finishing showing Mairead how to make an invisible join on a quilt binding.'

He hesitated, but was hauled into our midst and given a cup of tea whether he wanted it or not. He caused quite a flurry of excitement amid the sewing bee. His shirt was a token gesture, as if thrown on after a day in the sun. Only a couple of buttons were done up, and the sleeves were rolled tight across his strong biceps. Everything about Fintry glowed golden and his hair was white–gold, lightened by the sun. He could give movie stars a run for their money, though I supposed that Bredon was in the same tall, blond and sexy category.

Fintry thanked Ethel for the cuppa and wandered through to the kitchen area where Mairead was sitting at a sewing machine concentrating on getting her stitching straight.

She looked up and saw him. 'Fintry.'

'Don't rush,' he told her. 'I'll wait for you through here.'

'Take your time, Mairead,' said Ethel. 'We'll keep Fintry entertained, won't we ladies?'

Mairead laughed as Fintry was clasped eagerly into the hub of the bee.

'Will I ever get him back?' Mairead said to me.

I looked at them buzzing around him. 'Nope, you've lost him for sure.'

Mairead clipped the threads on the quilt binding, folded her work, put it in her craft bag and went to rescue him.

Ione sat in the kitchen using a knitting needle to stuff toy filler into the fairy doll she'd been sewing. 'It's lovely to be as happy and in love as those two.' She threaded a needle and sighed as she stitched the gap closed on the back of the fairy to finish the doll.

'Yes,' I agreed, 'it must be nice. I've only ever dated rotters. My fault of course for picking the wrong men. Not that I've dated many.'

'A friend of mine is like that,' said Ione. 'She's always broken hearted after falling for a stinker.'

'But you're happy with Sam, aren't you?'

'Very happy, but...well...I did fancy the beemaster even when I knew Sam. As an acquaintance. I guess that some men are a slow burn on the senses. I probably couldn't see how great Sam was because I couldn't see past Bredon. Now I can and I wouldn't have Bredon in a lucky bag. No offence, Aurora.'

'Why would I be offended? I'm not involved with Bredon.'

Ione shrugged and sat the fairy doll down on the table while she packed her sewing things away in her bag. 'You could end up falling in love with him.' She held up the fairy which was made from patchwork fabric in beautiful shades of blue. 'What do you think? This is my new fairy doll design. It's based on the blue Viper's bugloss flowers. I thought this would be the one I'd use for the magazine feature.'

'It's a fantastic design, Ione. And I love the vibrant blue colours. This is definitely going in the magazine.'

Her face lit up with the happiest smile. 'Thanks, Aurora.'

We wandered through to the living where everyone was packing up their sewing, knitting and crafts while watching Fintry and Mairead walking away.

'They're heading down on to the shore,' said Ethel. 'He had a look about him this evening. I wonder if everything is okay. He's never come to pick Mairead up from the sewing bee before. After all, their cottage is only just up the road.'

'It's a hot summer evening,' said Judith. 'He's probably taking her for a stroll along the sand.'

Ethel watched them out the window and frowned. 'No, he had a look about him. As if there was something he really needed to talk to her about.'

Hilda nodded. 'Yes, I think you're right, Ethel. If he just wanted to talk to her, he could do that at home in the cottage.'

Jessie picked up her bag. She was staying overnight at Hilda's house rather than sailing back to the island. 'He surely wouldn't be thinking of calling off their engagement.'

'He hasn't even set a date for the wedding,' said Hilda.

Ione dug her phone from her bag. 'I'll text her and ask if she's okay.'

Ethel pressed her hand on Ione's shoulder. 'No, I think they need a private moment to discuss whatever is on his mind.'

Ione put her phone away. 'We could follow them, spy on them, see what they're up to without being seen.'

'They'd see us,' said Ethel.

The other ladies agreed.

In hindsight, I should've kept my helpful suggestion to myself.

Although some of the bee members headed home, several of us left our bags at Tiree's cottage and followed my lead to go paddling in the sea. It was only a short walk down on to the shore and the sun still shone in the evening sky. A perfect night for paddling in the warm sea and for mischief.

The sense of mischief, of leaving our adult selves behind on the esplanade, caused Jessie to challenge Hilda to a childhood pursuit they hadn't attempted in years. I didn't encourage them. It wasn't my fault at all.

At first, Hilda was hesitant to take up her sister's challenge. 'Away you go, Jessie. We're not wee girls these days.'

Jessie's cheeks beamed with glee. 'All the more reason to let our hair down and have a laugh. Come on, Hilda. I dare you. I double dare you.'

'Well, in that case, you're on.' Hilda kicked her shoes off and pushed up the sleeves of her top.

'Don't let Jessie egg you on, Hilda,' said Ethel, looking concerned. 'It was always the same when they were younger,' Ethel confided to me. 'Jessie had no common sense and was always getting them into mischief.'

'I'm glad I'm not the only one stuck with the troublemaking label,' I told Ethel.

Ethel pursed her lips at me. 'There's a big difference between being a mischief–maker and a troublemaker, and you, young lady, are definitely the latter.'

By now Ione, Judith, Tiree and the others were watching the silliness unfold.

Ione shoved her phone in her bag. 'I've sent a text to Sam telling him I'll meet him later. This is too good to miss.'

Tiree nudged me. 'You're living up to your reputation, Aurora.'

'I only suggested we go down for a paddle so we could have a plausible reason to spy on Mairead and Fintry.' My defence sounded puerile, but it had seemed a good idea at the time I'd suggested it.

'We used to do ten cartwheels along the shore together,' Jessie explained to us. 'But seeing as we're not as fit as we used to be, we'll just do six.'

'No, the pair of you are being silly,' Ethel told them. 'And look, we're missing what Mairead and Fintry are up to.' She pointed to the two figures walking further along the shore.

Jessie brushed Ethel's words aside. 'Ach, we can still see them, and if he jilts her, we're right here to comfort her.'

Ione had a go at doing a cartwheel and ended up flopping down on the sand. 'I've never been able to do them properly,' she complained, brushing the sand from her clothes.

Jessie pushed up the sleeves of her cardigan to reveal a strong set of arms.

'You've got a fair load of muscles on those arms of yours, Jessie,' Judith remarked.

Jessie gave us a bicep pose. 'Years of helping my man on the fishing boats and working on the farm.'

Not to be outdone, Hilda gave us a show of her arm strength. 'All my quilting and ordinary hard work keeps me strong.'

'Okay,' said Jessie. 'Let's have a go.'

Jessie and Hilda lined up.

'You're both wearing skirts,' Ethel reminded them. 'You'll flash your knickers at everyone.'

By now, Hilda was well up for the challenge, and she was the one who brushed Ethel's remark aside. 'Knicker flashing on the shore is acceptable. That's what folk do in the summer.' She aimed her next comment at me. 'Flashing them at men, like the beemaster, is a different thing.'

I think Hilda was just winding me up, but there was no time to argue because the two of them started to do wild cartwheels across the sand. They were actually quite good at it. I was impressed. I was in Ione's league — rubbish at them.

We all cheered when they bounced to a triumphant finish, their faces beaming with joy. I was glad I'd interfered and that we'd gone down the shore instead of heading home from the sewing bee. This was what summer evenings were for — having fun, laughing with friends.

Jessie attempted to show Ione how to do a cartwheel, but they ended up in giggles on the sand.

'Here's Sam,' said Ethel, looking up to the esplanade.

He came bounding down the shore towards us. 'What are you lot up to?'

Ione got up and brushed the sand from her skirt. She smiled at him. 'Aurora suggested we come down here after the sewing bee to spy on Mairead and Fintry.'

Sam shook his head at me. I knew that expression. I was the troublemaker. He clasped Ione's hand, pulled her close and said to me, 'Look at the mess Ione's in. She's covered in sand.'

Without giving me a chance to explain, he put his arm around her shoulders and spoke gently to her. 'Come on, I'll run a warm bubble bath for you.' He glared at me and then ushered her away. She went happily, giving us a wave as she left.

'I wish a man would run a bubble bath for me,' Ethel muttered.

'I'm sure the postmaster would be delighted to oblige,' I said.

'No thanks,' said Ethel.

Hilda grinned at her. 'He'd let you handle his loofah.'

The others laughed, and for a few minutes we continued enjoying ourselves on the shore before heading home.

I looked along the coast. Mairead and Fintry had walked up on to the grassy verge and were now going back to their cottage.

A text message came through on Ethel's phone. 'It's from Mairead.' She read the message to us. 'We've set a date for the wedding. I'll explain the details tomorrow.'

'So that's what Fintry wanted to talk to her about,' said Judith. 'I wonder when they plan on getting married?'

'We'll find out tomorrow,' said Ethel. 'Remember, the film crew will be at Fintry's cottage. We can chat then.'

I drove home. The sun cast a mellow glow over the fields and countryside. Bredon's cottage was lit up and I saw him working outside at the beehives as I drove past in the distance. He didn't see me. A pang of longing went through me. I gripped the steering wheel and shook off the notion of how inviting his cottage looked — and the sense that it would no doubt feel great to be driving home to a man like him.

I got up early the next morning, bursting with energy and enthusiasm. I'd slept well and felt ready to tackle the day's work — and have afternoon tea with the dressmaker. Judith and Tiree would be there too.

It was another scorching day. I opened the windows and the front door and breathed in the warm sea air mixed with the scent of flowers and fields. I sat at my desk at the window and checked my emails. More patterns and photographs had arrived from some of the ladies including papercraft ideas to make a scrapbook. I nodded to myself. These were good. I set about editing and formatting them, then I went down to see what was happening at the flower hunter's cottage.

A small crowd had gathered, keeping a reasonable distance, to watch the film crew. A cameraman and two assistants, one of them a photographer, busied themselves, capturing Fintry at work.

Mairead saw me and waved. I waved back and went over to where Ethel, Hilda, Ione and others were standing, on the far side of the hedge overlooking the flower hunter's garden. They had a great view of everything that was going on.

'Fintry hasn't whipped his shirt off yet,' Ethel said to me, 'so you haven't missed anything. They've had him posing with his flowers as if he's working away.'

'I'm still not sure what this is for,' said Ione, brushing wisps of hair from her strawberry blonde plaits away from her pretty face.

'It's to advertise and promote Fintry's flower hunting book,' Ethel explained to her. 'Mairead's book publisher in London has organised it while the garden is looking lovely in the summer.'

'Have you had a chance to speak to Mairead?' Judith asked, joining us. 'Do you know when she's getting married?'

'Not yet,' said Ethel. 'Mairead whispered that she'd come over and speak to us once this load of photographs and filming is done.'

'I wonder if she'll be a snow bride?' said Hilda.

'No, look at them,' said Ione. 'They dote on each other. Why would they wait? No, I think they'll get married later in the summer or in the autumn.'

The women started to guess when the wedding would be, with the general consensus being the early autumn.

'The dressmaker has now hinted that she thinks there will be a wedding this year,' said Judith. 'I reckon she'll be right.'

Ethel nodded. 'Two weddings, if Tiree weds Tavion.'

'Phone me when you find out when Mairead and Fintry are getting married,' Judith said to Ethel. 'I have to be going. Tiree is helping the dressmaker finish a dress order that has to be posted off today. I'm on my way to the beemaster's cottage to photograph my tea cosy.' She had it tucked in her craft bag. 'He said I could drop by anytime and use his kitchen for the photographs. Will I include some that show Bredon's honey?' she asked me.

'Yes, definitely. And did you bake a honey cake?'

'I did. It's in the car along with the jars of honey. I used two tablespoons of the clear honey to make the cake. I thought if the jar looked like there was honey missing, it would be more authentic, as if someone really had baked a cake, and not just a fake set up for the pictures. What do you think, Aurora?'

'Great idea, Judith.'

Mairead signalled to us that she was coming round to chat to us while the film crew organised filming in another part of the garden with the lovely white cottage in the background. Judith waited with us.

'Well, when's the big day?' Ethel asked eagerly.

'Fintry said we could get married now,' Mairead told us. 'But I wouldn't have time to make my dress.'

'We'd all help you sew it,' said Ethel. 'And the dressmaker would run it up for you in jig time.'

Mairead sighed. 'I know that, and I appreciate it, but I want to look forward to planning the wedding. So then we considered having it in the autumn, but it's not my favourite time of year. Then we discussed getting married in the winter, which we both thought would be lovely. However, Fintry has to attend conferences down in London during November, so that only left December which is so busy with Christmas. We didn't want to get married at Christmas, so we've decided to get married in January, a year to the day we first met.'

'That's brilliant,' I said. 'It'll give you time to make your dress and look forward to everything.'

Mairead nodded enthusiastically. 'Exactly. I'm so excited about it. According to Fintry, it always snows here in January, and I love the snow.'

Hilda gave her a squeeze. 'You'll be a snow bride after all. It's magical getting married when everything is glistening white. Your dress and everything will sparkle like a fairytale.'

Ione squealed with delight. 'I'm all excited about it, and it's not even me who's getting married.' She gave Mairead a hug.

There were congratulations all round and then Judith said thoughtfully, 'If you and Fintry aren't actually getting married this year, then the dressmaker is wrong. She was right about a summer romance and engagement. However, she told me recently she had a feeling that a couple who live here would marry before the end of this year.'

We all looked at each other.

'And the dressmaker is never wrong, is she?' I said.

Judith was particularly perplexed. 'No, never that wrong. She's not one hundred percent accurate. That would be nonsense. But she's never that wide of the mark.'

'Someone else must be getting married,' said Ethel. 'It could be Tiree and Tavion. Or you and Sam,' she said to Ione.

'Me?' Ione looked surprised.

Ethel nodded. 'You two are at the bubble bath stage, so why not?'

Ione blinked. 'I hadn't planned on getting married to him. Not yet anyway.'

Hilda shrugged. 'It's either you or Tiree. No one else we know is even close to getting wed.'

Mairead became thoughtful. 'Maybe the dressmaker has her wires crossed. After all, I could've married Fintry this year. It was me who didn't want to rush things. Fintry only brought up the subject in case the film crew asked when we were getting married. He thought it was bound to crop up in the interview, and it has. He's on camera saying how we met at the cottage in the snow and making it our wedding date.'

Judith agreed. 'The dressmaker has been very busy this year with all the new dress designs, especially those for the film premieres. I wouldn't be surprised if she's got the date wrong for once. And it would only be by a month. If you'd got married at Christmas she would've been right.'

The film crew waved Mairead over to be included in the next part of the interview.

'I'll talk to you later,' Mairead said to us, and hurried over to chat beside Fintry.

We were asked to keep our voices down. We did, and listened while Fintry explained about Mairead introducing him to Franklin, her publisher. And then he mentioned the magazine.

'Mairead is working on a book of botanical illustrations, using the flowers in the garden,' said Fintry. 'Her artwork is exquisite — and she's included designs for quilting and embroidery in the book. And she's now using some of her floral art for a new online magazine that's being created here. It's launching soon, so she's sketching flowers from the garden while they're looking lovely. It's a grand summer this year.'

Ethel nudged me and whispered, 'Your magazine is getting a mention.'

'I know, that would be great publicity for it,' I said. 'Here's hoping they include it. It'll depend on what the press pick up on.'

'Here's Bredon,' said Hilda.

He came striding over to us with a loaf and a packet of biscuits in his hands. 'I was at the shops. What's happening here?'

I explained to him about the filming.

Fintry paused, said something to the crew, and then waved Bredon over to join them.

I held his shopping for him.

'This is the beemaster I was telling you about,' said Fintry. 'I've always encouraged bees and butterflies to my garden, and I plant flowers that are favourites with the bees.'

The crew were keen to discuss this aspect, and Bredon became part of the interview, talking about the types of flowers that people can grow for the bees.

Then Fintry and Bredon started laughing and took their shirts off, while the cameraman angled them into a corner of the garden where they were supposed to be working.

The women cheered and clapped, and were hushed by the crew.

Keeping our squeals of delight and giggles to ourselves, we admired two of the finest looking men in the community.

They only had their shirts off for a few minutes, then they put them back on, and Bredon came over to us, grinning at me.

'I didn't expect to get involved in the interview,' he said. 'I only came out for a loaf of bread and biscuits. I hope I didn't look like a prat.'

'No, you looked...' I hesitated. 'You looked fine.'

He smiled at me, and the intense blue of his eyes made my heart ache.

'Would it be okay to photograph my tea cosy in your kitchen?' Judith asked him. 'I baked a honey cake.'

'Yes, of course, Judith. I'm going home now.'

'I'm parked over there. I'll drive up behind you.'

He turned to me. 'Are you coming too?'

'I, eh...'

'Come on,' said Judith. 'You can advise me how to arrange the photographs for the magazine.'

And so I drove along with them. My heart was still fluttering, and I couldn't help feeling nervous about being near Bredon after seeing his toned torso and those fabulous blue eyes of his. I'd help with the photographs and then I had an excuse to leave as I was having afternoon with the dressmaker.

We parked outside Bredon's cottage and followed him inside.

'Arrange whatever you need,' he told us. 'I have to attend to the bees.'

'Is it okay if we make tea?' I asked him. 'We'll need it for the pictures.'

'Yes, and if there's a slice of cake going with it, that would be great.'

# CHAPTER SEVEN

## Afternoon Tea & Cake

Judith put her knitted bee tea cosy on one of Bredon's teapots. He had three teapots — one that he used regularly and two sitting on a shelf. One of those was a beehive shape and Judith used that one to display the yellow and brown cosy she'd knitted.

'What do you think?' she asked me, stepping back to admire it on the kitchen table.

'It's lovely. I like the yellow and chocolate brown striped pattern — and the bees to go with it.'

'I used Ethel's double knit yarn. The brown gives a nice warm tone with the pale yellow.'

We put Bredon's jars of honey on either side of the teapot and placed the honey cake in the foreground.

Judith had a camera with her, but I took pictures with my phone in case hers didn't turn out the way we wanted.

'I'll cut a slice of cake for Bredon,' said Judith.

I snapped some photos of the cake minus the slice which showed the delicious buttercream filling. The vanilla sponge and honey smelled yummy. Once the pictures were done, I hoped to indulge in a piece of it.

Bredon came in. 'How are you getting on? Oh, that cake looks tasty.'

'That slice is for you,' Judith told him. 'Do you want a cup of tea to go with it?'

He sat down at the table. 'I certainly do.' He bit into the scrumptious sponge cake. 'Tastes delicious, Judith.'

Judith beamed with pride.

While Bredon ate his cake, we tidied everything away, putting things back where they'd been.

'You're welcome to stay for lunch,' he said. 'There's no home cooking, but the cupboards have plenty of tins of soup, or you can make sandwiches.' He opened the fridge. 'I have lettuce, tomatoes, cheese, butter. Help yourselves.'

'We're actually having afternoon tea with the dressmaker, but would you like us to make you something before we go?' said Judith.

He grinned, as if the idea hadn't crossed his mind. 'I'll finish sorting the bees and be back in a few minutes.'

I opened the loaf while Judith sliced tomatoes, and together we prepared tasty cheese, tomato and salad sandwiches for him.

I poured the tea and went to cut myself a slice of cake.

Judith whipped it out of my hands. 'It'll spoil your appetite. The dressmaker will be offering you sandwiches, cake and ice cream soon.' She wrapped the cake up and left it for Bredon.

He bounded in, washed his hands and made my heart melt when he smiled at me. I blamed the summer. It made him look all golden tanned and luscious. I tried not to think about him with his shirt off in the flower hunter's garden. I did. I really did.

'Are you sure you won't join me for lunch?' he asked us. He sat down at the kitchen table.

'No, we have to be going now,' I said.

'Did you get the photographs you wanted?'

'Yes. Judith's tea cosy looked great on your teapot.'

He got up to see us out.

Judith waved to him as she drove off.

I got into my car and rolled the window down. 'Thanks again for letting us invade your kitchen.'

'Anytime, Aurora.' Then he said, 'I haven't had a chance to look for any photographs for my feature.'

'I've written a rough editorial based on information from your website.'

'Really?'

'Yes, and there are numerous pictures on the site we could use.'

'I'd love to read what you've written about me. Maybe you could come over for dinner tomorrow night and we could discuss the feature?'

'Okay. I'll bring the editorial and show you the photographs I have in mind to go with it.'

'Shall we say around seven?'

'I'll see you then.'

He smiled at me, causing a rush of excitement to charge through me. It wasn't a date, I told myself. It was dinner to discuss his feature.

I drove away, feeling the warm air waft in the window. Judith had suggested I follow her up the road to the dressmaker's cottage. It was a little early for afternoon tea, but she said it didn't matter. The dressmaker wanted to talk to me about the magazine and this would give us extra time to chatter before indulging in sandwiches and cakes.

The dressmaker's cottage was situated in the forest above the coast. When I was a young girl, I used to imagine it was a magical forest filled with secret niches. The branches of the trees arched across the narrow road. The greenery, with carpets of bluebells and other flowers, created a misty effect. I caught a glimpse of the beautiful bluebell garden cottage tucked into its own little niche, surrounded by bluebells and fairy lantern flowers. It had a water garden with a starwort stream that trickled down the pathway towards the fields far below. Blue lilies wafted in the breeze and I recalled many a happy day playing around here. It was a holiday home now and rented out for the summer.

As I drove towards the dressmaker's cottage, I felt a pang of trepidation. The dressmaker was as sharp as the pins she used for her sewing and didn't suffer fools. I would need to be careful not to cause any trouble.

The first thing I noticed when I parked in the driveway was the sense of another era. The traditional, two–storey cottage belonged to the past, as did many of the cottages in the area, but this one had a vintage quality and a magical atmosphere. The garden merged with the surrounding forest and the greenery was deep and lush. The richness of the plants produced a heady aroma and the tall thistles seemed to stand on guard along the edge of the driveway, offset with the pretty colours of the mesembryanthemum flowers whose leaves sparkled in the sun as if sprinkled with starlight.

I parked beside Judith's car and followed her inside the cottage.

'I think Bredon fancies you,' Judith said, leading me through to the living room where the dressmaker sat at a table working on one of her designs. Tiree's sewing machine whirred away in the background in the adjoining sewing room. Shelves of fabric covered the pale blue–grey walls and created an extraordinary decorative effect.

The dressmaker smiled at me. 'And do you fancy the beemaster?'

I laughed nervously.

'Answer enough,' the dressmaker concluded, giving me a wry smile. She looked quite lovely. She was of retirement age and very pretty, wearing an exquisite vintage–style drop–waist dress, made by her no doubt. I thought her elegant blonde chignon looked especially nice.

'Ione does our hair,' she said, as if reading my thoughts. 'Isn't that right, Judith?'

'Yes. We decided to go a bit glam recently for a film premiere event,' Judith explained, 'and we're keeping it that way with regular colour touch–ups.'

'It's very flattering,' I said.

The dressmaker smiled and invited me to sit down at her table that had a view of the garden through the patio doors. Thimble was stretched out in the sunshine.

Judith put her bag down. 'I'll start preparing the sandwiches and tea.'

She disappeared into the kitchen, leaving me to chat to the dressmaker while Tiree called through, 'Did someone mention tea?'

'And sandwiches,' Judith called back through to her.

'I've almost finished this dress,' said Tiree. 'Then I'll come through to join you.'

The dressmaker relaxed back in her chair and had a good look at me. 'You look as beautiful as ever — but unhappy. Soul weary. What happened to you in London?'

'I grew up.'

'Did you cause as much trouble down there as you used to cause here?'

'Is there any point in lying?'

She laughed lightly. 'I don't know everything. I can't see right through you.'

Her pale blue eyes contracted her last remark.

'I don't try to be a troublemaker,' I emphasised.

She nodded. 'It's part of who you are. And it's not up to you to try to be what you're not. It's up to us to accept you for what you are.'

Judith carried through a tea tray. 'Nothing but trouble.' She grinned at me and started to set the table with cups, saucers, plates and silver teaspoons.

Tiree came through, tidying her hair that had fallen loose with the effort of her intense sewing. 'I thought I was the troublemaker around here.'

'You lost your crown the day Aurora came back and reclaimed her title,' said the dressmaker.

Tiree gave us a pretend pout. 'I'll just have to try harder.'

'Don't you dare,' the dressmaker scolded her. 'We had enough trouble with you and Tavion before you realised you were made for each other.'

'Fair warning,' Tiree said to me. 'They're up to their matchmaking tricks again. No single young women are safe from their finagling.'

'Remarks like that, Tiree, will not get you a slice of my home made chocolate cake,' said Judith.

The banter was light–hearted and made me feel at ease in their company.

Judith had been right about not eating anything to spoil my appetite. We had salmon sandwiches, chocolate cake, butterfly cakes with whipped cream and peach slices and pots of tea. This was followed by tall glasses of lemonade and ice cream eaten outside in the garden patio. We chatted about Tiree's romance with Tavion, handsome men, designer dresses and the magazine.

'Have you decided to move in with Tavion yet?' the dressmaker asked Tiree.

'He's hinted a few times and asked me outright, but I'm not sure. I love living at the strawberry jam cottage. Tavion's house is great, and it's surrounded by his flower fields, but I'm reluctant to give up the wee cottage.'

'It was always going to be temporary accommodation,' Judith reminded her.

Tiree understood. 'It was part of the job perks, living in the cottage. I know that. I just want a bit more time to think about it.'

'That's fair enough,' the dressmaker admitted. 'But be careful not to let your chances of real happiness drift.'

Tiree turned the spotlight away from herself and on to me. 'What about you and the beemaster? There's been a lot of gossip — and alleged knicker flashing.'

'Bredon hasn't flashed his knickers at me once,' I said.

They laughed.

'He's invited me to have dinner with him at his cottage tomorrow night.' I explained that it was to discuss the editorial for his feature.

'We'll see if any sparks of romance flicker between the two of you,' said the dressmaker. 'And speaking of an editorial feature, I'm interested in advertising in your magazine. Judith tells me that all the adverts are written as features.'

'That's right,' I said. 'I'd be happy to include your dressmaking. And thank you for contributing a dress pattern.'

'I have the pattern ready. I'll email it to you before you leave today. Judith says it's handier for you if I email everything.'

'Yes, it's quicker than having to retype all the features. I can edit and format everything for the online issue.'

'I'd be lost without my laptop,' the dressmaker admitted. 'It's so handy for resizing my patterns, and the world is at my fingertips. I rather like it.' She went to go inside to get it, but Tiree ran in and brought it out.

'Thank you, Tiree.' The dressmaker opened the laptop and accessed her pattern files and templates. 'While you're here, Aurora, I'd like to show you what I have in mind for the dress pattern. Although it's a wrapover tea dress, I've designed it in three templates to fit most sizes. Would this work for your website download?'

I hadn't anticipated how technically adept the dressmaker would be. 'This is wonderful. Thank you. I'll convert this so that readers can print out the different pattern pieces in the sizes they need.'

The dressmaker looked delighted. 'Great. I was hoping this would work.' She paused and then said, 'When I first heard that you were going to publish a magazine I thought it was a frivolous notion. Then I realised it could work. It's great for the community. Everyone's getting involved. I feel as if this is something special. Judith showed me the pagination sheet you gave her, and when I read the contents you plan to include in your magazine, I thought — I'd read this.' She frowned. 'It's very ambitious of you, but very feasible if you work hard. And I believe you will. In fact, I think you need to relax sometimes. I've heard all about you working through the night.'

'It's difficult when there's so much work to be done,' I said. 'But once the first issue is launched, I should be able to pull back on the throttle. I'm also trying to compile the second issue, adding features that aren't suitable for the first issue but still of interest.'

'I understand how hectic work can be. There are times when I have to work continuously to finish a dress order for a special client.' The dressmaker smiled at me. 'Just keep in mind what I said. And enjoy having dinner with the beemaster. There's nothing wrong with mixing business with pleasure.'

I sipped my lemonade and smiled. 'You're all a bad influence on me.'

The dressmaker lifted her glass and proposed a lemonade toast. 'Here's to the success of Aurora's magazine — and plenty of love and laughter for us all.'

The four of us clinked our glasses, sitting round the patio table in the sunshine and making plans for the dressmaker's feature.

Judith's photographs turned out brilliant and she emailed a copy of them to me. I said I'd crop them and choose the best ones for the feature. She also emailed the tea cosy patterns.

By the time I left, it was early evening.

I drove down the winding forest road, catching glimpses of the sea through the trees in the distance. When I arrived at my cottage I was able to access the emails and start formatting the features with the photographs and pattern templates. I didn't even have to make dinner. After eating sandwiches, cakes and ice cream, I was fuelled up for work.

I sat down at my desk, opened the living room window and let the warm air drift in.

Far in the distance boats sailed along the coast, into the harbour or further out to sea heading for the islands. I wondered if the filming at the flower hunter's cottage had gone well, and what sort of publicity Mairead's publisher in London would drum up from it.

And I saw Tavion working in one of his flower fields. Would Tiree make the jump and move in with him? Would he ask her to marry him first? As I looked around I realised that a community like this could be a hive of activity, even compared to London. There were so many people whose lives intertwined. Cottages were dotted for miles along the coastline, or like the dressmaker's cottage and the bluebell cottage, hidden up in the forest, or situated in the fields like Tavion. Then there was me, in my cottage, perched on the edge of the hillside.

I settled down to start work. I adjusted and cropped Judith's photographs. The bee tea cosy pattern fitted well into the feature leaving plenty of room to highlight Bredon and his honey. I printed a copy of the double page spread to take with me to show Bredon. The other tea cosy Judith had knitted, the lovely sparkly turquoise one, tempted me to extend the knitting to another double page spread. This would provide readers with two knitting patterns for cute cosies and let me write more about the beemaster. I paused. Was I inclined to give him extra editorial space because I liked him? Or was it because his work and the photographs of his beehives and garden merited it? Maybe a bit of both, but there was something really appealing about the amber honey, the flowers in his garden that were planted to attract the bees, and the photographs in his kitchen. It was the perfect feature for the magazine, and so I decided I would give it extra coverage. An online issue allowed me more leeway to increase pages without affecting the cost as a print issue would.

I also added the dressmaker's tea dress pattern along with the written instructions on how to sew it. The pattern was fairly straightforward which was what I wanted for the magazine — great patterns that were achievable. This dress would work well for various levels of sewing experience. The dressmaker had included sketches — fashion illustrations drawn in pen and ink of the finished design. Tiree promised to sew the dress and take pictures for the feature, but I also wanted to incorporate the dressmaker's illustrations.

On the pages following the dress pattern, I added Tiree's collar templates. Then I put Jessie's gold work embroidery and cross stitch patterns, followed by Ethel's features on dyeing and spinning yarn, and her lace weight shawl knitting pattern. The colours of the yarn were fantastic.

I finally stopped working when the sky was filled with twinkling stars.

A single light shone from one of the windows of Bredon's cottage. His garden was lit with fairy lights. All the little beehives looked like something out of a fairytale.

Tomorrow night I would be there, perhaps sitting outside in the garden, chatting to Bredon about his business and my magazine. Would either of us consider adding pleasure to the mix?

The dressmaker's words filtered through my thoughts as I flicked the lights off and climbed into bed by the glow of the night. *And do you fancy the beemaster?*

Yes, he was one of the most handsome men I'd met, but was I ready to drop my guard and let my heart become vulnerable again?

Bredon wasn't the type of man I could have a summer fling with. Not that a fling was my sort of thing. Summer romance tended to fizzle out. The last thing I needed was another broken heart, especially as I intended settling down here.

I set the alarm on my phone and was just about to put it on the bedside table when a text came through — from Bredon.

'I noticed your lights were on late. Are you still up?' he asked.

'No, I'm sleeping.'

'Sweet dreams, then.'

I went to settle down, but now I wanted to know what he wanted. I sent another text. 'Was there something you wanted to talk to me about?'

'Dinner. I wanted to know what you'd like to eat. I'm really not very adept at cooking. Even less experienced at entertaining company like you. Any suggestions?'

'Buy in food. I'll cook dinner.'

'No, I invited you. Any other options?'

'Sandwiches?'

He sent me a smiley. Then he replied, 'Dinner in a restaurant? We could still discuss the feature.'

'No, I'd prefer to stay at home rather than eat out.' I pressed the send button and then gasped when I realised I'd referred to his cottage as home. I squirmed, waiting on his response.

'Me too. Let's compromise. I'll buy in food and start dinner. If all else fails — sandwiches.'

'Agreed.'

'See you tomorrow night, Aurora. Goodnight.'

'Goodnight.'

I put the phone aside and breathed a sigh of relief. Hopefully he hadn't noticed my silly comment.

Several minutes later another text popped through from Bredon. My phone alerted me.

'Are you still awake, Aurora?'

'Nope. Fast asleep.'

'I meant to ask — how did you get on at the dressmaker's cottage this afternoon?'

'I had a nice time. And I won't have to eat for a week. I'm totally stuffed with chocolate cake and ice cream.'

'That'll save me cooking dinner.'

I smiled to myself.

We said goodnight again, and then I finally settled down and went to sleep.

# CHAPTER EIGHT

## Vintage Scraps & Seahorses

I worked on the papercraft features in the morning. I had fresh fruit and a cup of tea for breakfast, and my stomach fluttered every time I thought about having dinner with Bredon.

The scrapbook feature instructions had arrived by email. The photographs of the book were gorgeous. It had been made from vintage–style scraps with seahorses and starfish, entwined with ribbons and lace. I fought the urge to get out my scissors and use Mairead's beautiful artwork scraps to start making one myself.

I continued working through lunch and into the afternoon, making the day go in, putting the magazine together, waiting until it was time to drive to Bredon's cottage for dinner.

I wore a little silk dress, kept my hair down, and took my satchel with me filled with the page samples to show him.

His cottage was aglow with lights as I parked outside. Lamps shone inside the living room, and the garden looked magical lit with fairy lights. The night air was warm and my heart beat nervously as I walked up to the front door. It was open and I saw Bredon rushing around. He wore dark trousers and a dark blue shirt. His hair was damp and smoothed back from his face. He looked like a man who'd just showered, dressed classy but casual, made an effort to have everything ready for dinner, and was probably as anxious as I was.

'Aurora. You're here.'

'Eh, yes. Can I help with dinner?'

'Yes. I've sort of got everything organised, but I've made a complete arse of it as well.'

'It smells delicious, whatever it is.'

The temperature in the kitchen was scorching. I was sure his hair would be dry within minutes. Both ovens of his cooker were on. He opened the top oven. 'Does this turkey look as if it's ready?'

He'd roasted a turkey? In this weather? It smelled delicious and the outside was crisp and golden. 'It looks ready.'

He turned the heat down, closed the oven door and then checked the small oven where a selection of vegetables were sizzling in a roasting pan.

'Roast potatoes?'

'And parsnips, carrots and onions,' he said. Then he lifted the lid off a pot on the hob. 'And Brussels sprouts. They're frozen, but I peeled the roasties myself.'

I tried not to smile.

'Say it, go on, say it, Aurora.'

I shook my head.

He flicked the kettle on and started to make gravy and a pot of tea. I helped him. I kept my lips pressed shut for as long as I could, but when I saw him carving up the turkey and dishing out the roast potatoes and vegetables, I laughed.

'What?' he said.

I shook my head again.

'Come on, just say it.'

I wiped away a tear of laughter and pointed at our meal. 'This is Christmas dinner.'

'Ho, ho, ho.' He sounded slightly annoyed. 'I thought I'd cook a turkey. I'm quite okay at roasting stuff in the oven. It generally cooks up fine. Then I thought — potatoes, and I had a rifle through the freezer and found frozen veg and suddenly once it was all sizzling away I realised I'd rustled up a festive fiasco.'

'It is, but I've hardly eaten anything all day. I'm hungry, so this is perfect. Except for the heat. It's stifling in here.'

'We could eat Christmas dinner outside in the garden.'

And so we did. We sat outside and ate dinner by the glow of the fairy lights.

'This is very tasty,' I told him.

'I'm sure Ethel, Judith and the other gossips will enjoy hearing about it.'

'I won't tell them.' This was probably a lie.

'Of course you will. They'll want to wring out every detail from you. What did he make for dinner? What were you wearing? Did he kiss you?'

I gasped.

'You know what I mean.'

'I told them we were having dinner to discuss your feature.'

He smiled and continued to eat his meal.

While we ate dinner we chatted about the magazine. After he cleared the plates away and I'd teased him about there being no

Christmas cake or mince pies to go with our tea, I showed him the editorial I'd written.

He brought his laptop outside and sat beside me so I could point to the photographs on his website that I wanted to include in the feature. A couple of times I caught him looking at me rather than at the computer screen. I felt myself blush and was glad that we were sitting outside in the glow of the evening.

'Is there anything you want me to change in the feature?' I said.

'No, what you've written is excellent. I wouldn't change any of it. I notice you've even included a list of flowers to create a bee garden.'

'The information was on your website. I thought readers would be interested.'

He got up. 'I have something for you that you might like.' He went into the cottage and came back out carrying an old–fashioned book. He handed it to me.

'This looks lovely. What is it?' I went to open it.

'Careful. The pages are filled with pressed flowers. I picked a selection of the bees' favourites from the garden today and put them between the pages of the book.' He shrugged. 'I hope you like it.'

'I love it.' I opened the pages slightly to take a peek. Pretty pink petal daisies with yellow centres were pressed inside.

'Those are daisy fleabane.' He indicated other flowers in the book. 'Those are chocolate daisies. And teasel, bluebells...all sorts of flowers.'

I smiled at him. 'Thank you, Bredon. I used to press flowers in paperback books when I was a girl. I'd pick flowers from the cottage garden and press them. Then when they were dried, I'd make them into pictures. We had a couple of them framed and hung up on the walls. I don't know what happened to them. I guess they were thrown away when the cottage was modernised.'

'Maybe you can make some new pictures with these flowers.'

I held the gift in my hands. 'Yes. Where did you get the book?'

'I pick things up wherever I go, particularly at conferences. This was a large notebook. I liked the old–fashioned design and creamy coloured pages, as if the book was from a bygone era. It's not. But it has that traditional design.'

I tucked the book into my satchel along with the samples of his editorial. 'Thanks for dinner.'

'Would you like to take a look at the beehives before you go? The garden is rather magical at night.'

I left my bag on the chair. 'Okay.' He led me over the lawn to two of the hives. The garden felt so calm, the air still and warm. A perfect summer evening. He clasped my hand and helped me step over the little stone path that separated the lawn from the hives. The fairy lights and a couple of solar lamps illuminated the darkness, but I was glad to have him steady me.

Fronds from the bee garden flowers brushed against my bare legs, but it was the feeling of Bredon's strong and capable fingers wrapped around mine that sent tingles through me.

He could've let go of my hand when we stood beside the hives, but he didn't. He pointed to the different sections of a hive with one hand while keeping me close to him. Too close.

I tried to listen to what he was telling me, but it became harder to concentrate as I tried to control the beating of my heart. In the quiet night air I was sure he would hear my heart pounding.

In my mind I knew I should ease my hand away from his, and yet I didn't want to. I wanted to feel his hand holding mine in this magical bee garden on a hot summer evening when the fields around us were quiet and it felt as if there was just the two of us.

'...And that produces a really delicious honey.' His words were suddenly back. He waited on my response.

'That's totally fascinating,' I lied, not wanting to offend him.

'It's part of the reason why I love my work.' He smiled down at me. His handsome features were highlighted in the evening glow and his hair tempted me to run my fingers through it.

He turned to face me full–on, focussing all his attention on me, rather than the bees.

We gazed at each other for a moment and then he pulled me close, leaned down and kissed me.

Everything in my world tilted as he pressed his smooth, sensual lips against mine, and I gave in to the temptation, returning his kisses with all the passion I felt for him. My fingers felt the silky texture of his blond hair and I wrapped my arms around him. My hands trailed across the nape of his neck, and then moved down to feel the strong muscles of his broad shoulders and back underneath the fabric of his shirt.

We stood there, forging our feelings for each other together. He pressed his body close to mine, merging the contours of his masculinity against me.

I finally pulled back, worried I was making a mistake, making promises I wouldn't keep.

'I have to go,' I said breathlessly.

He gently brushed my hair back from my face and kissed me, sweetly.

I picked up my bag from the chair, and my legs felt quite wobbly as I walked to where I'd parked my car. I hoped he didn't notice, and if he did, he'd credit it to the uneven ground as I made my way through the bee garden.

His words followed me. 'I didn't intend to kiss you tonight, Aurora. I wanted to. I've wanted to kiss you since I first met you. But I promised myself I would be on my best behaviour this evening.'

'We all break promises to ourselves,' I said, looking back at him. 'It's the promises we break to other people that matter more.'

We obviously hadn't made any promises to each other. However, potential lovers could promise everything with a single kiss.

I drove off, feeling elated, confused, slightly breathless and totally convinced I wouldn't sleep a wink that night when I got home and went to bed.


In the morning I made my way down to Ethel's cottage to show her the editorial for her yarn and knitting feature.

I'd always liked Ethel's cottage — the blue painted walls and flowers growing around the door. I knocked at the front door and was surprised when Mairead opened it. She had a concerned expression and spoke in a hushed tone.

'Ethel's very upset. She got a letter from her granddaughter, Glen, this morning. The news took her aback. She phoned me and I came straight over. Hilda's on her way too.'

'I remember Glen.' I didn't try to disguise my dislike of her. We'd never been friendly, mainly because Glen had a hoity–toity attitude to things she deemed beneath her, which included me. Glen was a few years younger than me and from what I'd heard, she'd become a model and was now training to be a fashion designer. I didn't doubt she'd achieve all that she aimed for. Glen was...well, not ruthless, just selfish to the core.

'Glen's been messing Ethel around for months,' Mairead confided. 'She tells Ethel she'll turn up to visit, then cancels at the last minute. Ethel thinks the world of her, and Glen knows this.' Mairead shook her head in disgust. 'I've never met Glen and I have no wish to do so.'

'What did she say in the letter? Has something happened?'

'Glen got married a couple of weeks ago. She sent the letter from New York.'

'New York?'

'She's back from her honeymoon in Hawaii and living in Manhattan. Apparently she's married a rich young businessman who is heir to a fashion chain.'

'I'm sure Glen loves him dearly.'

'It'll cost him, that's for sure.'

'And Ethel knew nothing about this?'

'No. It's a real slap in the face. Ethel didn't even know Glen was dating this man. She thought she was dating some musician in a band and had no plans to wed. She let me read the letter. What a stinker Glen is. She even included a wedding photograph showing her cutting the cake. It seems to have been a lavish wedding in London. Ethel could've been there, but Glen didn't invite her.'

'That's just nasty.'

'It is, so you can understand how upset Ethel is. It's come as a shock.'

'Do you think it's better if I come back later?' I said.

'Is that you, Aurora?' Ethel called from the living room. 'Come away in.' Her voice was shaking with emotion.

I went in to see if I could comfort her. She was sitting in her chair, looking like a broken soul. Her eyes were swollen from weeping. I could've wept for her, but I didn't want to upset her further.

I crouched down beside her and gave her hands a squeeze in mine. 'Is there anything I can do for you, Ethel?' My words seemed futile but my offer was genuine.

'Yes,' she murmured. 'Punch Glen's chops for her if she ever has the cheek to show her face here again. I'm done with her. Done. Selfish, selfish girl.'

'I'll kick her scrawny arse from here to Auchtermuchty,' I promised.

Ethel's teary eyes looked at me and she put her hand on top of mine. 'Thanks, Aurora.'

Mairead went through to the kitchen to make tea and I heard her make a whispered call to Fintry, letting him know what had happened.

'How did you dinner date go with Bredon?' Ethel asked me, trying to focus on something else rather than Glen.

'It went well. I had a lovely time.' I certainly had.

'What did he cook for your dinner? What did you wear?'

I smiled to myself remembering what Bredon had said the ladies would ask.

'I wore a nice silk dress. It was a hot night.'

'In more ways than one?' Mairead called through from the kitchen.

I laughed. 'Maybe.'

'Ooh!' said Ethel. 'Did he kiss you?'

I laughed lightly.

Ethel smiled. 'I knew it.'

Mairead carried the tea tray through and put it down on the table.

'We want all the details, don't we Mairead?' said Ethel.

'Yes. What did Bredon end up cooking for dinner? He phoned Fintry for advice and seemed in a tizzy over it. He's usually so easy–osey. I think he was really nervous and wanted to impress you with his culinary skills.'

I poured the tea. 'I was impressed all right. He'd roasted a turkey — with sage and onion stuffing.'

Ethel blinked. 'Roasted a turkey? In this weather? The kitchen must've been stewing.'

'It was. I was glad I'd worn a silk dress. He'd also roasted potatoes and cooked other vegetables including...Brussels sprouts and parsnips.'

Mairead frowned. 'That sounds like...'

I nodded. 'Christmas dinner.'

'What was he thinking?' said Ethel.

I shrugged. 'He said he was quite okay about roasting a turkey and then everything else accidentally turned into Christmas dinner, with gravy by the way. The veg were frozen from the freezer. I really think he didn't do it intentionally.' I started to laugh and so did they.

'And did you eat it?' Mairead asked.

'I did. I was starving. I'd been so worked up about going there I hadn't eaten anything substantial all day. We ate outside in the front garden because it was cooler.'

We were giggling when Hilda arrived. Her hair was all over the place. 'I ran all the way from the post office when I heard the news about Glen.' She flopped down on a chair opposite Ethel. 'Are you okay?'

'I was upset, but Mairead and Aurora have cheered me up.' Ethel told Hilda about Bredon's dinner effort.

Hilda shook her head. 'Men. They're worse than weans sometimes.'

'And there was kissing,' Ethel added.

Hilda eyed me, wanting details. They all wanted details. Luckily I was saved from revealing what happened near the beehives when Fintry arrived at the cottage. The door was open and he ventured in.

'How are you doin', Ethel?' he asked her.

'I phoned and told him about the letter,' Mairead explained.

The letter was lying on the table beside the tea tray with the wedding photograph on top of it.

Hilda leaned over and studied it. 'Her wedding dress looks like pish. Calls herself a fashion designer — blah!'

Mairead poured Fintry a cup of tea.

'So are you up for a sail along the coast, Ethel?' he said.

'Sailing?' Ethel gasped. 'On your yacht?'

Fintry nodded. 'It's too fine a day to go to waste. I thought you'd like to come with Mairead and me. I'm taking a trip along the Forth. We'll be back in the late afternoon. It'll do you good. Blow all the badness away.'

Ethel looked taken aback and yet I could see she was tempted. 'I've never been on your boat, Fintry.'

He drank his tea down. 'Then it's about time you were. Come on.'

'What should I wear?' said Ethel. She wore a skirt, top and flat shoes. Similar to what most of us were wearing. I had a dress on and comfy pumps. So did Mairead.

'What you're wearing is ideal,' Fintry told her. He reached out, took her hand and pulled her to her feet.

Ethel seemed flustered. 'What about food? Will I rustle us up some sandwiches and cake?'

'There's no need,' he said. 'The galley's stocked with all we need for munching. Though if you have any of that tasty shortbread of yours, that wouldn't go amiss.'

Ethel hurried through to the kitchen to get it. 'I've got a full tin we can take with us.'

Fintry gave us a knowing wink. A kind soul, I thought.

Ethel grabbed a cardigan, a shawl and her bag.

With Ethel on one arm and Mairead on the other, Fintry led the way out of the cottage. 'Come on, you two. Are you not coming with us?' he said.

'Me?' said Hilda. 'On your posh yacht?'

'And you, Aurora. If you're not too busy working on the magazine.'

Hilda and I exchanged an excited glance. Sailing on a gorgeous sunny day up the coast on the flower hunter's big yacht, or working? No contest.

We all headed down to the harbour and after assuring Ethel that we had plenty of milk on board to make tea, we set sail.

I glanced back at the shore. High on the hill I saw my cottage. I smiled and relaxed back on the seat on deck, watching the sun strike off the water, clear green and blues, and listening to the excited chatter of Ethel, Hilda and Mairead.

At the helm, Fintry seem strong and capable — and happy to have us with him.

I would remember this day we sailed together, leaving our troubles on the shore, and heading out to sea in the beautiful Firth of Forth.

We anchored off the coast of a shore, whose sand was so white it looked like silver, to have lunch. Although it was simple fayre of sandwiches, cakes, tea and Ethel's shortbread, it tasted extra delicious on Fintry's yacht. The sense of freedom as the water lapped off the hull of the yacht was a memory I would keep forever — that and the friendship we all enjoyed and shared that day.

I took photographs with my phone, as did the others.

As we sailed along again, Ethel said to me, 'So, what happened when the beemaster kissed you last night?'

Hilda's eyes widened. 'There was snogging? We thought there would be. Is he a sexy kisser?'

The women giggled.

'Close your ears, Fintry,' I called to him as he stood at the wheel, turning the yacht around. 'This is gossip and girl talk.'

'What was that you said, Aurora?' he joked.

I laughed and started to tell them everything that had happened during dinner with Bredon, minus a few private details that I was sure their minds would imagine anyway.

As we sailed back home the sea near the islands was particularly gorgeous. Ethel gazed at it. 'The colours are wonderful. It's put me in the notion to dye some yarn in those shades of sea blues. Maybe it's the sunlight, but the intensity of the colours is beautiful.' She turned to Mairead. 'As a watercolourist, what would you call those shades of blue? They're not teal or ultramarine. I've got yarn in those colours. These are really lovely.'

Mairead looked out at the sea. 'Prussian blue, Antwerp blue, cerulean and manganese.'

'You can write those down for me when we get back,' Ethel said to her. 'I'll add them to one of my collections.'

Fintry sailed the yacht into harbour and we stepped ashore.

Ethel smiled at Fintry. 'I can't thank you enough for taking us sailing with you. I thoroughly enjoyed myself.'

We all thanked Fintry and then I walked back up to where I'd parked my car. Hilda went back to Ethel's cottage, and Mairead and Fintry headed home too.

I drove along the road thinking about the grand day I'd had — and about Bredon.

I saw him in the distance, kitted out in his white beekeeping gear, working at the hives. He didn't see me, and I drove on, needing to unwind from the day's heady events and to think what I was going to do about him.

Emails were piled up in my inbox. Lots of new patterns and projects had arrived. I kicked my shoes off, poured a refreshing glass of mineral water with lemon and lime, and started work again on the magazine.

The low rumble of thunder rippled across the darkening sky. I gazed out the window. A summer storm was heading inland. The sky was streaked with purple and violet.

I kept the windows open. The air felt electric and a sense of excitement swept through me. As a girl I'd always loved to sit in the safety of the cottage and watch the thunder storms rage across the sky.

A flash of lightning tore across the coast, illuminating the islands in the distance, glinting like a mirror, signalling a powerful storm brewing.

# CHAPTER NINE

## Bumblebees by the Sea

I snuggled up in bed and watched the rain sweep along the coast, drenching everything in its path. I'd seen storms like this before at the height of summer. I sensed the warm spell in the weather was about to break, washed away for yet another year, giving way to the fading warmth of the summer.

When I stepped outside the cottage the next morning, the air was warm, not hot. The temperature had dropped slightly. It was still a lovely day and everything was fresh and clean from the previous night's downpour. Tavion was out working in his flower fields. His flowers had withstood being battered by the rain, but he was harvesting a large section of a field, assisted by a couple of young farm workers.

I sipped my mug of tea and watched the boats sail out to sea, then I saw the figure of Bredon outside his cottage, attending to the bees, looking as busy as they were.

My phone rang. It was Mairead.

'I've just had a call from Franklin in London,' she said urgently.

'Is something wrong?'

'Yes. One of his top editors, Sebastian, has released pictures from the photo shoot with Fintry. He's sent them to a couple of his contacts in the press.'

'Wasn't that the intention?' Was I missing the point? They wanted media publicity.

'It was, but Sebastian has gone ahead and given them the photos and a rough of the press release that Franklin hadn't finished approving. They were supposed to discuss it and finalise the details before the press release went out from the publishers.' Mairead sighed in exasperation. 'Sebastian's got a reputation for doing things like this. He's worked with Franklin for years, even though he's around the same age as Fintry. Franklin thinks of him as the troublesome son he never had. Sebastian has a unique talent for being brilliant and for stirring up trouble.' She was kind enough not to mention I'd understand that label.

'Has Franklin contacted the press? Explained to them what's happened?'

'He tried, but they've already run with the story. Both newspapers. The reason the press were so eager is because Sebastian slanted the story, making it more newsworthy was his excuse, and he gave them the photos of Fintry and Bredon with their shirts off. One of the headlines is something like — a flower hunter and a beemaster strip off in the wilds of Scotland in heritage garden. Another part of the story is — local ladies go wild for naked flower hunter and beemaster.'

'Oh.'

'Exactly.'

'Does Fintry know?'

'Yes, he was out on his yacht but he's sailing back now.' She paused. 'Someone's going to have to tell Bredon.' I could tell by her tone she didn't want to.

'I'll tell him.'

'Thanks, Aurora. I'll email a copy of the stories to you. Franklin gave me a link to them. Hang on while I send them to you.'

I waited a moment and then I heard the ping as they arrived on my laptop. I accessed the stories. 'The photos are...extremely flattering.'

'And sexy as hell,' she said bluntly. Which was exactly what I was thinking.

'At least Fintry and Bredon look fit and handsome. I know it's not what was intended, but this will ensure quite a bit of publicity for Fintry's forthcoming book for Franklin. And sales of Bredon's honey could go up.' I was searching for the good points.

'Read down to the part where it mentions about your magazine. Sebastian has taken a huge liberty. He's said the magazine is a new online issue, about to launch, and that Franklin is part of it.'

My eyes scanned the screen. 'Jings!'

'Jings indeed.'

I read some more and my eyes widened when I saw that it mentioned the dressmaker.

'Have you seen the bit about the dressmaker giving one of her special designer patterns?'

'I'm reading it now. Oh jeez, how did they get that information?'

'I emailed Franklin a copy of the updated pagination sheet so that he could see the contents of the magazine. I included the dressmaker's pattern as this is the first time she's ever let anyone see one of her pattern designs. Franklin's got a fashion book coming out soon. I did a few of the illustrations. It seemed relevant. But Sebastian has used the pagination sheet information. What a mess.'

I thought for a moment. When I worked for the magazines in London, life was rarely smooth. I often had to adapt, move fast when opportunities arose and duck and dive the harsh stuff. 'Not if we turn things around and use it to our advantage.'

'Can we do that? The magazine isn't ready to be launched.'

'No, it's not, but it could be. It would be a lot of hard work, but it's feasible.' I could scarcely believe I was even considering launching the magazine early. This early. 'The most difficult thing about launching this type of magazine is gaining publicity for it. I couldn't afford this type of media publicity. It's like gold dust. I have to take advantage of it.'

'I'll help, and I'm sure the other ladies will too. I'll rally the girls — if you tell Bredon he's pictured without his shirt on in the newspapers.'

'I'm sure he'll just love that.' My tone was heavy with sarcasm.

Before Mairead hung up she said, 'There's something horribly exciting about this fiasco.'

I agreed with her, though first I had to pop down to Bredon's cottage before I could think how to pull things together for the launch.


Bredon smiled cheerfully as I parked outside his garden gate. His bees sounded extra lively in the morning air. Maybe they sensed that trouble had arrived.

He stepped forward, unsure whether or not to kiss me.

I held up a copy of the newspaper article I'd printed out to show him.

He blinked several times as the information sank in. Even in the printout there was no disguising that his bare–chested physique, along with Fintry's, had been highlighted under the main headline. I hadn't realised his trousers were so low on his lean hips. When he'd bent down to supposedly attend to bees on a plant in the flower hunter's garden, a hint of his bare bum was showing.

The press hadn't missed it though. A caption mentioned *bum*blebees.

He sat down on a garden chair and I gave him a moment to read the article.

'It wasn't my fault,' I said. How many times in my life had I uttered that phrase?

His trusting blue eyes gazed up at me. 'I was the one who took my shirt off.' He shook his head in dismay. 'I thought with the publisher handling the publicity it would be more subtle, tasteful.'

I explained about Sebastian.

'So what are you going to do?' he asked.

'Rally the girls and get this magazine finished, polished and press the launch button. I can't undo the damage this may have caused to your reputation, but I can redress it by publishing a great feature on you and your bees in the magazine. You've seen the editorial. You liked it.' I tapped a finger on the printout. 'This will be chip paper by tomorrow. The magazine feature will stay relevant and be online for months.'

He put the printout aside and pressed his hands firmly on his thighs. 'What can I do to help?'

'Make your cottage available for photographs. I have numerous items, such as quilts and a sewing machine cover, which has a bee theme by the way, that need lovely settings for the backdrop. My cottage is okay but nothing special. Your cottage and your garden is perfect for the photo shoots.'

'You're welcome to use it.'

I beamed at him. 'Thanks. This could work.'

He stood up, towering above me, his handsome face gazing at me against the clear blue sky, trusting me.

'I'd better get started.' I hurried to my car.

'And I'd better get ready to be invaded by the ladies and their crafts.'

'It could be worse,' I called back to him.

'How so?'

'You and your beemaster cottage could be inundated with visitors from other towns and cities, especially ladies, wanting to see you in your natural habitat. To catch a glimpse of your...*bum*blebees.'

'I could arrange a private viewing for you.' He gave me a sexy grin.

'Be careful. I might take you up on that offer — and you can imagine what sort of trouble that could lead to.'

He laughed as I drove off.

I headed home and concentrated on the magazine while emails and frantic phone calls tried to interrupt my determination to edit like blazes.

By the afternoon I realised a number of photographs were needed to complete lots of the features. I phoned around and organised as many of the crafters as possible to meet me at Bredon's cottage and to bring their items with them so we could take the pictures. If even half of them turned up, I knew it would be another chunk of the magazine complete.

When it was time, I headed down to Bredon's cottage, having pre–warned him we were on our way.

I arrived about ten minutes early. I wanted the chat to Bredon, to reassure him that no matter how many quilts, sewing machines, knitted items and papercraft work was set up, the mess would be tidied when we'd finished.

'I popped down to the shops and stocked up with milk and biscuits,' he said. 'Then I plan to work with the bees. I'm certain they'll be less busy than you and the ladies.'

I didn't argue that fact.

We were outside in his garden. The beep of a car horn signalled the arrival of Judith. The car windows were rolled down and Ethel, Hilda, Tiree, Ione and even Mairead were inside waving out. The vehicle juddered to a halt outside the front gate and they began unloading themselves and the craft items.

'I'm surprised they didn't bring Thimble the cat with them,' Bredon muttered and then disappeared behind his beekeeping hat to work at a hive.

'Jessie's sailing over on her husband's boat,' Judith said to me. 'She'll be here within the hour. She says to tell you she's bringing her quilts, embroidery and tapestries with her.'

'What do you need us to do?' said Mairead.

'While the sun's out, hang Hilda's quilts and her wee quilt blocks on the washing line,' I said. 'Judith? Have you got your camera with you?'

Judith dug it out of her bag.

'Start taking photographs of the quilts from various angles. Try some with the cottage and the garden in the background,' I said. 'And take some with the hills and Tavion's fields as the backdrop.'

Judith couldn't wait to get started and I left them to organise the quilt pics while I sat Ione's new fairy doll beside the daisy fleabane flowers and sweet peas that were growing in the garden. I snapped several shots. 'What do you think?' I said to Ione, giving her a look at the pictures on my camera's preview screen.

'Oh, the colours are lovely, Aurora.' She took something from her bag. 'I don't know if you'd be interested, but this is my new seahorse softie.'

'Perfect. Sit him beside the flowers and I'll photograph them together.' I took several snaps.

Ione dug deeper into her bag. 'And this is the dressmaker's cat softie.' She held it up. The face resembled Thimble with fabulous green eyes and an upright tail that gave him attitude. She propped him up beside a beehive.

At that moment I heard Ethel talking to Bredon, asking him if it was okay to give Thimble a saucer of milk when she made tea for everyone.

Bredon cast a look over at me. I said nothing.

At the mention of milk, the cat meowed from inside Judith's car. He was stretched along the back seat.

'Judith,' I called. 'Do you think you could bring Thimble over to have his picture taken with Ione's stuffed toy version of him?'

Judith nodded, scooped up the cat who was quite happy to be lifted, and brought him over. He sat quite the thing beside the softie. It was probably just a fluke, but I managed to capture a shot of Thimble looking as if he was smiling, sitting next to his stuffed double. I hadn't intended including a black cat pattern in the magazine but I thought it would work really well.

Other ladies arrived with their items, including Jessie, and soon Bredon's cottage and garden was abuzz with chatter and craft activity. We photographed almost everything we needed. Only a few items were missing, and if necessary, I planned to leave those out of the launch issue.

I'd brought my laptop with me and kept checking the pictures on screen to see they were suitable for the magazine. We kept going until the sunlight started to fade, but then I realised how beautiful the bee garden was at night, first at twilight, then later all lit with fairy lights. I even snapped a couple of extra pictures of Ione's fairy doll — a night shot that looked magical.

Judith had cooked Bredon's dinner for him, though we'd gone through his food cupboard supplies like a bunch of termites. Bredon didn't seem to care about this and was happy to be fed and fussed over.

As the ladies headed home I warned him, 'We'll be back again tomorrow morning.'

'That's fine. It's like a manic holiday break. Jessie even brought me a candyfloss up from the shop down the shore. And Judith has promised to bake me a steak and beer pie with puff pastry for dinner tomorrow.'

'Spoiled rotten.'

'Indeed I am.' He stepped closer. 'So, do you really have to go now?'

'I do. I've a ton of editing to finish. And I'm going to make a start on formatting the photos we took.'

'Another long night and into the wee small hours.'

I nodded and on tip–toes gave him a quick kiss. 'See you in the morning. Early start.'

I worked on the magazine until I nodded off at the computer. I closed the laptop, tumbled into bed and slept right through until the morning.

I jumped in the shower, threw on a casual navy and white print cotton dress, and thought I'd be the first to arrive at Bredon's cottage. I was wrong. Ethel was there cooking sausages, bacon and eggs for his breakfast. He sat at the kitchen table and smiled at me as Ethel handed him a plate of the delicious cooked breakfast and offered him hot buttered toast to go with it.

'Toast for you too, Aurora?' she said.

'Thanks. I hadn't even thought about breakfast. My mind was in editorial mode.'

'I've brought my new yarns with me — the deep blues, purple, magenta and the fuchsia. I've also selected the amber and gold double knit shades.'

'They'd look lovely with a vase of chocolate daisies. Would you mind if we pick some of the flowers?'

'Help yourself,' he said, tucking into his food.

I ate my toast, drank down a cuppa, and then cut a variety of flowers from the garden and arranged them in teapots, jugs and vases in different parts of his house.

Ethel draped skeins of yarn over the washing line so we could see the vibrant colours in the bright daylight. The morning was fresh and clear.

The three of us were in the garden when Mairead arrived looking distressed. 'I have bad news and rotten news.'

I gripped tightly to the bunch of daisies in my hand. 'What's the bad news?'

Mairead took a deep breath. 'Sebastian is on his way here. Franklin sent him to make amends for the trouble he's caused.'

'What can Sebastian do?' I asked her.

'Cause more trouble no doubt,' said Mairead. 'Franklin means well, but Sebastian is a complete arse. He's the reason that Daisy, the botanical illustrator who worked for Franklin in London, ran off to Cornwall. Daisy dated Sebastian and he cheated on her horribly with Franklin's daughter, Celeste. Daisy is happy now in Cornwall and is well rid of Sebastian, but that's not the point.'

'Sebastian sounds like a right womaniser if you ask me,' Ethel commented.

'He is,' said Mairead.

'What's the rotten news?' said Bredon.

Mairead looked disheartened. 'Sebastian will be here soon. He caught the first flight out of London to Edinburgh. Big Sam has gone to pick him up at the airport. Sam had a furniture delivery to make in Edinburgh, so he's picking Sebastian up in the van. Fintry offered to go but I was worried he'd throttle Sebastian for the chaos he's caused.'

'Maybe you should've let Fintry go and throttle him,' said Bredon.

Mairead nodded. 'One thing's for sure, at least one of us will want to throttle Sebastian before he goes back home to London.'

Bredon frowned. 'How old is Sebastian? Franklin's age?'

'No, he's a lot younger,' said Mairead. 'He's about your age. A successful young businessman. He's Franklin's top editor and meddler extraordinaire. And suave, sophisticated and probably sexy if you like men in suits who love themselves.'

'Perhaps we should phone Sam and tell him to drop Sebastian off somewhere else,' I said.

'The ferry to Skye on the west coast,' Bredon added. 'And abandon him there.'

I started to laugh, which caused the others to join in.

I smiled at them. 'Maybe a dose of us is just what Sebastian needs.'

'Especially from a troublemaker like you, Aurora.'

'Thanks, Ethel,' I said, wondering how bad this Sebastian chap could be.


The other ladies arrived, and while we were out in the garden taking photographs of Ethel's yarn and other craft items, Sam's delivery van drove up. We heard it before we saw it. Sam's rock and roll music and his loud, cheerful singing, blared from the van. A man in his early thirties wearing an expensive grey suit, white shirt and tie got out of the van the moment it was parked. He carried a laptop bag.

Sebastian had arrived.

I went over to meet him. His face was exceptionally handsome with stunning eyes that looked like they never missed a trick. His light brown hair was well–cut and as smooth as his grey silk tie. I hated that I found him devilishly handsome.

Mairead introduced us. 'Sebastian, this is Aurora. As you know, she owns the new magazine.'

Sebastian cocked his head. 'I'm sorry, could you repeat that, Mairead? My ears are still ringing from the dulcet tones of Big Sam's enthusiastic singing — all the way from the airport.'

Oh yes, I thought. Sebastian was going to be difficult.

Sam jumped out of the van. 'He hardly ever joined in.' He dumped Sebastian's large suitcase on the grass.

*Hardly*? Sebastian had been singing along with Sam?

Sebastian gave a disdainful look. 'Had it been Chopin's Polonaise, I might have been more inclined.'

Sam frowned. 'I don't think I know that song.'

Ione came running over and gave Sam a huge hug. She squeezed his strong biceps. 'Did the delivery go okay?'

'Yes,' said Sam, 'and Sebastian here gave me a hand.'

I guffawed. 'Sebastian helped you lift the furniture?'

Sam nodded. 'He's stronger than he looks. I dropped off two sofas on the way back from the airport. Sebastian helped me lift the sofas up the stairs to the flat I was delivering them to.'

'Consider it part payment in penance for creating national news coverage in the press for Aurora's new magazine, Franklin's publishing company, and Fintry and the beemaster's businesses that's worth its weight in gold.'

Mairead ignored Sebastian's remark and continued to introduce him to the others. 'And this is —'

Sebastian extended his hand to Bredon. 'The beemaster. Sorry about your bumblebee being splashed across the papers. Totally unintentional. Hope it sells more of your honey.'

Bredon shook hands with him. 'It's certainly created quite a buzz. Thankfully Aurora is prepared to exhaust herself trying to launch the magazine weeks before she planned to.'

Sebastian turned his gaze to me. 'I apologise profusely for any trouble I've caused.'

I found it unusual to be on the receiving end of those words.

Sebastian then turned his attention to Ethel's yarn, draped over the washing line. 'Lovely colours.'

'I spin and dye my own yarn,' Ethel told him. 'Are you into any crafts?'

'Nooo,' Sebastian emphasised. 'I'm more into shops. Those places where I buy things that other people have had the time and inclination to make for me.'

Mairead's eyes flashed angrily. 'You're being a total arse, Sebastian.'

He didn't flinch. 'Mairead loves me really, especially when I use her botanical illustrations rather than someone else's to accompany the editorial in the books Franklin publishes.'

He had her on that one. Mairead had told me how grateful she was that Sebastian often used her work, and that he was the one who recommended her to Franklin when Daisy deserted them. Certainly, he was the cause of Daisy running off and never coming back, but Mairead's career had benefited. Often this was due to Sebastian.

Mairead's work merited being used in the publishing company's non–fiction books, however, Sebastian had been good to her.

She didn't retaliate. She didn't smile at him either. Instead we all started to get on with our business again, leaving Sebastian to flounder.

Unfortunately, Sebastian was made of stern stuff and made himself at home, relaxing on a garden chair and accepting a cup of tea and slice of cake from Judith.

'He's a handsome rotter,' Tiree whispered to Mairead and me.

'Hopefully he'll sod off back to London soon,' I said.

'I'm here for a couple of days,' Sebastian called over to us.

Had he heard our conversation? Or was he just really good at sussing situations? Probably the latter. Whenever I looked at him I felt uneasy. He was a handsome one. But a rotter and troublemaker to the core.

# CHAPTER TEN

## Fairytale Designs & Stargazing

Later in the day Mairead had started sniping at Sebastian. 'You're the one who cheated on Daisy. You're the reason she left London.'

'Huh! That's old news. I've caused heaps of trouble since then.' He was now sitting with his feet up on a lounge chair in the garden enjoying the sunshine. He'd taken his jacket off, though his shirt and tie remained immaculate. Another cup of tea had been served to him along with one of Judith's home baked cherry muffins.

He glanced at the cake after taking a bite. 'What am I eating? It tastes like cardboard.'

'Cardboard,' Mairead told him. 'You're supposed to peel the thin cardboard paper off the edges.'

Thrawn to the last, Sebastian swallowed the remainder of the morsel he was chewing. 'I've tasted worse.' His fabulous eyes stared at me. 'After I've digested this delicious cardboard cake, what can I do to help you?'

Again, I loathed myself for finding him attractive. As I didn't reply, Mairead muttered, 'Go back to London.'

Sebastian ignored her comment and continued to talk to me. 'You're obviously the ring master of this circus, Aurora. I've been watching, and you've certainly got plans for this exciting new magazine with all these pretty pictures, but surely there's something I can do to help. Remember, I'm a damn fine editor.'

And a damn fine looking man. And horribly likeable. There was something appealing in his unshakable arrogance. Or perhaps the remnants of my life in London were affecting my senses. Yes, that's what it was. Sebastian reminded me of all the things I'd left behind, including men like him.

Sebastian picked up a pagination sheet that was lying on the grass. He started reading it. He took his time, digesting every detail, reading it as an editor would, considering all the aspects of the contents.

I kept working, arranging the handmade jewellery one of the ladies had made, setting it on a wooden table with pieces of sea glass and flowers. I arranged it so the jewellery caught the sunlight. The blue, green and amber sea glass matched the colours in the flowers. But all the while I glanced at Sebastian, wondering what he thought of my contents plan.

Finally, he stood up and came over to me. 'This is first–class. Even I'd read this magazine.'

I hadn't realised I'd been holding my breath. I let out a huge sigh. 'Thanks. I was wondering what you thought of it.'

'I've never worked on magazines,' he said, 'but I've worked as a non–fiction book editor for years, so it's the same sort of arena. I particularly like the idea of advertorials, making every page readable in that sense, without quarter or full–page ads or box ads. That's an audacious move. I'm surmising you're trying to up the readership and intend making your money from actual sales of the mag rather than the advertising revenue?'

'Yes. I'm selling advertising as advertorials for the magazine. I'm also having normal ads on the website. Readers will be given patterns and templates for everything from embroidery to papercraft and colouring in sheets that they can download from the website, so advertisers will benefit from the exposure there.'

Sebastian kept nodding. 'I really like this. If this fails, which it won't if you can keep the issues published monthly, you should come and work with Franklin and me in London. You'd have a ball. You and your ideas and your editorial experience would fit right into our world. Think about it.'

Bredon hurried over. 'Aurora is happy doing what she's doing.'

'Everyone in business should have options,' said Sebastian. 'The market changes all the time.'

'Aurora has recently left London to settle here,' said Bredon, putting his arm around me.

'That means she's the type of woman who makes bold decisions and will up sticks to wherever she wants to be.' Sebastian cast a glance at Bredon's arm. 'Or perhaps your motives for wanting Aurora to stay in Scotland aren't entirely selfless.'

Dark clouds started to drift in from the sea and a cold breeze suddenly blew away some of the flowers beside the jewellery, ruining the arrangement for the photos. A shiver went through me.

'I think it's going to rain soon,' I said. 'We should call it a day and meet here again tomorrow.'

Everyone gathered their things.

'Your steak pie is heating in the oven,' Judith told Bredon. 'It'll be ready in about ten minutes. Don't let it dry out. There's plenty of gravy under the puff pastry. I made the gravy with real ale. It adds flavour.'

'Thanks, Judith. It's ages since I had a proper home cooked dinner.'

Sebastian observed Bredon. 'You're like one of your hives, with all the busy little bees buzzing around you at your beck and call.'

'It's only because the ladies are here using the cottage for the photos,' said Bredon.

Sebastian sniffed, as if he disapproved. 'It would be so easy to mistake who was using who.' He strutted over to the lounge chair and put his jacket on. 'Can anyone recommend a local hotel or bed and breakfast? I'll be here for couple of days.'

Sam had arrived to pick up Ione. He overheard Sebastian. 'You're out of luck this time of year. During the holidays everything is booked up. There's no hotel for miles anyway, just local bed and breakfast, or people willing to take a stranger in for the night.'

'So, I'm sleeping rough, on the shore. Is that what you mean?' Sebastian asked.

Sam shrugged. 'I'm just saying, you'll not find anywhere available like you're looking for. I'd normally offer to put you up for the night, but Ione's staying the night with me. She likes to skip around in the noddy, so I can't let you get a free ogle.'

'Perish the thought,' said Sebastian.

'I've got a spare room,' said Ethel, 'but I won't have a man sleeping under my roof under any circumstances, even if you could afford me.'

Sebastian smirked. 'I'm convinced you don't come cheap, Ethel.'

No one else made any offers. No one wanted Sebastian.

'I suppose I could put you up for the night.' Bredon's tone was completely unwelcoming.

Sebastian shook his head. 'No. You'd probably stuff a beehive or a hornet's nest under my duvet while I was asleep. It wouldn't be worth the nightmares.'

'Oh for goodness sake,' I said, 'I have a spare room. You can stay at my cottage.' I pointed to it on the hill.

Bredon's face looked as thunderous as the sky.

'Don't worry,' I assured Bredon. 'If Sebastian steps out of line, I'll punch his lights out.'

Bredon glared at Sebastian. 'And she's a trained boxer. Aurora packs quite a punch.'

Sebastian smiled casually. 'I love how welcoming you all are.' He smiled at me. 'Okay, shall we head home before it buckets down?'

Spits of rain sprinkled through the air.

We all scattered, and I drove Sebastian to my cottage.

Sebastian gazed down the hill. 'The beemaster will be tucking into that steak pie by now.'

I invited him into the living room. 'Your bedroom is through there. I'll start making dinner.'

'Don't you have editorial to do?'

'Eh, yes, but I'm hungry. All that fresh air. And somehow I haven't had a proper meal, just loads of tea and a slice of cake. It's been a busy day.'

Sebastian took his jacket off and put his suitcase and laptop bag down. 'You edit, I'll cook dinner.'

'You can cook?'

'I can cook up a storm.'

As he said this a flash of lightning illuminated the living room, making me jump.

Sebastian laughed. 'Seriously, you start processing the pics, formatting more pages and I'll rustle up dinner.'

I went to show him where things were, but he sat me down in the living room.

'I can find my way around a kitchen, Aurora. Now, let's get this magazine ready to launch.'

Within an hour Sebastian called through to me, 'Dinner's ready.'

I eased the muscles in the back of my neck, stood up and wandered through to the kitchen. He'd set the kitchen table and whatever was cooking smelled amazing.

He sat me down and poured me a glass of red wine.

'Where did you find this?' I said.

'Lurking at the back of a cupboard on a shelf you're not tall enough to reach without a climbing rope and crampons.'

I laughed and eyed the contents of the glass with suspicion. 'It could be off.'

'Taste it. If you keel over gasping, I'll know it's not for me.'

'You're a vile charmer, aren't you?'

'A passive–aggressive compliment?' He considered it for a moment. 'Yes, I suppose I am. Is that so bad?'

'Probably.'

He started to serve up the meal. 'I raided your freezer, fridge and cupboards. You're not into cooking, are you?' Then he reconsidered. 'Or are you just unsure of where you are?' He nodded. 'Yes, you're unsettled here.'

'It doesn't help that I have to go like laldy to get the magazine out.'

'My fault I suppose.' He put down a dish of mixed vegetables that had been kept warm in the oven while he cooked the pasta and made the tomato and red pepper sauce to go with it. 'Everything is always my fault even when it's not.'

'That makes a change for me.'

'Ah yes, you're the trouble magnet.'

I glanced at him.

'Ethel, Hilda, and I'm sorry I don't know all the gossips' names, mentioned this to me.'

'Then you'll understand, being a trouble magnet yourself.'

'All the more reason why we should stick together.'

'No. Double trouble? Bad idea.'

'I'll tell you what was a bad idea, on Bredon's part.'

'What?'

'Letting you leave with me.'

'Bredon doesn't tell me what to do.'

'You're in love with him.'

'Who told you that?'

'He did, when he put his arm around you and glared daggers at me. You were comfortable with him doing that.'

'We're just getting to know each other.'

Sebastian sprinkled freshly ground pepper over the pasta sauce. 'If I'd been him, we'd be sharing that steak pie and puff pastry. I definitely wouldn't have let you spend the night with me. That's really asking for trouble from two known troublemakers.' He shook his head. 'I'd have held on to you with hoops of steel.'

'Don't do this. Don't try to make me doubt Bredon.'

'Okay, I'll behave.'

'Tell me about you and Daisy. Did you use your wily charms on her? Did you love her?'

'I did. I messed up big style. I went down to Cornwall to try and win her back. It didn't work. I'd behaved appallingly and she wouldn't forgive me.'

We continued to chat over dinner about publishing and magazines, and then Sebastian set his laptop up in the living room and together we tore through the editorials. He was right about one thing — he was a damn fine editor, and it was nice having someone to share the workload with. We bounced ideas off each other.

I was through in the kitchen at around two in the morning making tea while Sebastian edited a feature.

'Can you decipher Morse code?' he called through to me.

'Is that for Ethel's knitting feature?'

'No. Bredon's flashing signals at us with a torch. He's flicking it off and on.'

'Is he?' I hurried through and peered out the window. The rain had stopped but the night looked cold and damp from the downpour earlier. Bredon was at his bedroom window and signalling up to the cottage.

I phoned him. 'What are you doing?'

'Telling you to get some sleep, and hoping Sebastian hasn't caused you any trouble.'

'I'm working late but finishing soon. And Sebastian has been very helpful.'

'He hasn't tried it on with you?' Bredon sounded jealous. 'I don't want to sound like the jealous boyfriend.'

Sebastian overheard him and couldn't resist making a stupid remark. 'Aurora, come to bed. It's late. I've heated your side of the bed.'

Sebastian thought this was funny. I didn't.

I blame being tired, very tired for what happened next. When my fist punched Sebastian's face it wasn't supposed to hit him hard. I only meant to give him a slap on the jaw to warn him to shut up. Unfortunately, we clashed. I threw the punch as Sebastian stepped closer.

'Are you okay?' Bredon shouted, hearing the stramach.

'Yes, everything's fine. I'm going to bed to get some sleep — alone. Sebastian is in the other bedroom.' Needing an ice pack for his eye.

I hung up.

'Am I going to have a black eye in the morning?'

I checked the damage. 'Maybe, but there's no real damage done. It's your own stupid fault.'

He got up and headed through to his room. 'At least if the magazine fails miserably, you've got a back up career in the boxing ring.' He closed the door and that was the last I heard from him until the morning.

Despite having a mild black eye, Sebastian still looked handsome. Showered and wearing a clean shirt and tie, he'd made breakfast for us.

'Stop making me feel guilty,' I said, tucking into my omelette.

'I'm lathering on the guilt today.' He sat down opposite me and started to butter his toast. 'I couldn't sleep, so I got up again and edited the other features you were working on. All done.'

My cutlery clattered on my plate.

'Consider it my parting shot before I leave.'

'You're leaving today?'

'The welcoming mat was never really out, was it? I'm catching a flight from Edinburgh. Stay in touch though. And the offer to come and work in London is still open.'

After breakfast Sebastian's suitcase was packed and he was ready to go. 'You've got another subscriber to add to your list.' He pointed to my laptop.

I went to check my email. 'Who is it?'

'Me.' He smiled, and I heard to toot of a horn outside. I assumed it was his taxi. 'I phoned around this morning but there were no taxis available — except for one.'

I peered out the window. Sam's van was parked outside.

'Silversmith, delivery man, tone deaf singer.' Sebastian picked up his things and headed out.

Sam smiled. 'I've got that song you mentioned. It doesn't have any words, just fancy music, but we can just sing la, la, la to it as we go along. You can join in this time seeing as you know the tune.'

91

Sebastian forced a grin. 'Joy of joys.' Then he climbed into the van and off they went.

I breathed a sigh of relief.

During the next few days I worked to finish the magazine and have it ready to launch. Everyone gathered at Bredon's cottage. I wanted to share the launch moment with all those who had been involved. There was a party–style atmosphere in Bredon's living room that evening. Glasses were filled with whisky, sherry and ginger wine.

We raised our glasses and drank a toast to the magazine. And then I pressed the button on my laptop that made the magazine live. A cheer went up. The room was bursting with friendship and laughter.

'That's it out there in the world,' I said, sounding a bit emotional. It had been a hard week of long hours, trying to pull it all together, backed to the hilt by friends old and new.

'What now?' the postmaster asked me.

'Issue number two.'

Another cheer went up. Thankfully, I had a lot of it done already. Features from the first issue had spilled over into the second, either as a follow–up, or because they were better suited to a later issue due to the content. The newspaper publicity had certainly drummed up interest, and the number of subscribers who were interested in a new craft magazine had shot up. The media fiasco had also benefited Fintry and Bredon. Both of them had been offered various deals from companies and individuals who'd read about them in the papers. And Franklin was delighted with the pre–sales orders for Fintry's flower hunting book and for Mairead's illustrated book with its floral quilt blocks and embroidery motifs and patterns.

So all was well with the world. Especially if people enjoyed reading the magazine. Jaec Midwinter the chocolatier was at the launch party and asked me if he could have a double page advertorial featuring his new chocolate recipes. I was happy to do that. He'd given his permission for us to use his chocolate topping recipe for Ethel's cake in the first issue. And he'd been kind enough to bring a large chocolate cake masterpiece for everyone to share at the party. We took photographs of it before it was decimated. The ladies were now in the habit of taking pictures of anything magnificent that could be used for the magazine.

I looked over and there was the chocolatier expertly cutting the cake while Judith, Tiree and Ethel put the slices on to plates and handed them round. No one refused a slice of the chocolate confection. Bredon balanced two plates and brought them over.

He gave one to me. 'Well done, Aurora. I'm proud of you.'

'Thanks for letting us invade your cottage for the photographs,' I said.

'It's going to be so quiet again here. I think I'll miss the company — one person especially.' He gave me a loving look and was about to kiss me when Sam came bounding over to us.

'Are we jigging? There's no room in here but it's a grand night outside for dancing on the front patio and in the garden. What do you think? Will I get the music sorted?'

'Yes, let's do that,' said Bredon.

Sam bounded away to get it organised and soon the party spilled out into the night.

I slow danced with Bredon, enjoying the way he pulled me close. 'I'm so glad you left London and came back here,' he said. 'I can't imagine never having met you.'

I felt the same about him. I hadn't known him long, but I felt I knew him well and didn't like to think what I'd be doing if I hadn't come back to Scotland.

As the music and our laughter drifted into the air, I gazed up at the night sky, so clear and filled with stars. 'It's a beautiful night.'

Bredon wrapped me in his arms. 'And beautiful company.'

After midnight, everyone headed home, leaving me alone with Bredon. I ended up staying with him, snuggling up, just snuggling, until the morning.


A few busy days later I went to the sewing bee in Tiree's cottage. We'd all started sewing, knitting and crafting new projects, most of them for the next issue of the magazine.

I was working on the dressmaker's tea dress pattern using a fabric printed with bees and butterflies. Tiree showed me how to piece it together so that it fitted perfectly. Tiree had also been helping Mairead design her wedding dress. Mairead had drawn sketches of her dream dress and Tiree was making these work as a pattern. They were using cream silk to sew a toile, keeping the dressmaker's oyster silk fabric for the finished garment. Mairead agreed that I could feature her wedding dress design in the magazine, month by month, leading up to the actual wedding in January. Mairead was delighted to have an archive of each step of the design process of the dress, and I was sure readers would be interested in it. From the initial sketches, the dress looked like it was going to be fit for a fairytale snow bride.

At the end of the sewing bee evening Tiree made an announcement. 'Before you all go, I have to tell you that this is the last sewing bee I'm having here.'

A disappointed gasp went up.

'No, it's fine,' Tiree assured them. 'I'm still continuing the sewing bee, but the next one will be at Tavion's house.'

'You're moving in with him?' Ethel gasped and then smiled.

Tiree's cheeks flushed but she seemed pleased to be telling us her news. 'Yes. We've been talking about getting married. And before you think that we're the couple getting married this year, we're not. I don't want to hurry it. We're planning on getting married next summer. I want to look forward to it.'

'So,' Mairead said, 'you're engaged. It's official.' She sounded so happy for Tiree.

'I haven't got the ring yet,' Tiree explained. 'I'm such a slow–coach when it comes to deciding things like that. Tavion is taking me to the city to trail round all the jewellery shops.' She pressed her palm against her chest. 'I'm so excited. I've always wanted to do the 'going round trying engagement rings on thing' and making a day of it in the city. We'll probably go to Edinburgh or we might drive across to Glasgow.'

I was delighted for her. 'Maybe both. Really make a day of it. Or two days.'

We all gathered Tiree in our arms and gave her a group hug. By the time we'd squeezed the breath from her, her hair looked like she'd been walking along the coast on a blustery day. No one cared, least of all Tiree. Squeals of excitement for her happy news, along with the prospect of invading Tavion's house during the sewing bee evenings, filled the cottage.

'I don't even know what type of ring I want,' said Tiree.

'You've got lovely slender fingers,' Hilda observed. 'You'd suit a trilogy ring — three diamonds in a row glistening on a pure gold band.'

'Or an emerald–cut design,' suggested Jessie.

'A fairytale style,' said Ione, 'with lots of sparkly diamonds.'

'What about a vintage ring?' said Judith.

I threw my thoughts into the ring. 'Or a diamond cluster.'

'Better tell Tavion to take a flash of tea with him for the shopping trek,' said Ethel, smiling. 'Luckily he's fit and strong, but I've seen fitter men wilt when they have to shop until they drop.'

'I've warned him' said Tiree, 'but he hasn't stopping grinning at me since I told him I was moving in with him. The big sapsy.'

'That means the strawberry jam cottage will be vacant again,' said Hilda. 'I wonder who'll move in next?'

'The cottage lease belongs to the dressmaker,' said Judith. 'It'll be up to her who gets it.'

'Tell her we want another handsome man,' said Hilda. 'All the stoaters are getting taken.'

We laughed.

Ethel eyed Ione. 'If Tiree and Mairead are marrying next year, does that mean it'll be you and Sam tying the knot this year? The dressmaker thinks someone will.'

'No,' Ione insisted. 'Not this year. I'm like Tiree. I want to take my time. I do love him and we're likely to get wed, but certainly not yet.'

With our thoughts brimming with engagement rings and wedding dress designs, we left Tiree's cottage for the last time. She waved us off. 'Remember. We'll meet at Tavion's house next week.'

The week went in quicker than I thought. I'd been busy with the new issue and enjoying time with Bredon. I felt so comfortable in his company, even when he kissed me with such passion he took my breath away.

I'd been having dinner with him most evenings, including the night of the sewing bee.

We sat at the kitchen table finishing our meal.

'The sewing bee is being held at Tavion's house now. This will be our first night there,' I reminded Bredon.

'I spoke to him earlier today. All he talked about, apart from his flowers, was Tiree. He's a happy man.'

'They're a fine couple.'

'As are Fintry and Mairead. Two engagements this summer. I can hardly keep up with the romantic gossip.'

He started to clear the dishes away while I got my things ready for the sewing bee. My craft bag sat in the living room, and when I went through to pick it up, I noticed a pad and pencil with bumblebee sketches on it.

Bredon came through and saw me looking at them. 'I wanted to talk to you about this.'

'The sewing bee doesn't start for half an hour. What did you want to tell me? Did you draw these?'

'I'm no artist, not like Mairead. These are just some ideas for designs I have in my mind. I scribbled them down and wanted to know what you think?'

I assumed they were for a new label for his jars, or a logo for his website. 'What are the designs for?'

'For a ring.'

'A ring?'

He nodded.

'What for?'

'For you.'

'Me?' My voice sounded like a high–pitched squeak.

He picked up the sketches and flicked through them. 'I had this idea to make a ring, shaped like a bee, encrusted with diamonds and set in gold. Maybe two shades of gold. I asked Sam, with him being a silversmith, if he could make something like this and he said he could. So, if you'd like a bumblebee or a honey bee on your finger, I'll commission Sam to make it. He'll size it to fit whatever finger you want to wear it on.'

My heart beat excitedly. 'Whatever finger?'

'Yes. It would be up to you. No pressure. And even if you wanted to wear it as a token of my affection, with potential for it to be more, I'd be happy with that. Of course, should you choose to wear it on your ring finger, I'd be the happiest man in the world.'

I gasped when I realised what he was asking.

He nodded. 'I'd marry you this summer, this autumn, whenever you wanted.'

I needed to say the words to make sure they were real. 'Marry me?'

'Yes. Perhaps the bee design is a silly notion, but I've never met anyone like you, Aurora. You're unique. I thought you'd like a unique ring.'

I gazed at the design. Yes, now I could see where he'd drawn the diamonds. Lots of fair–sized diamonds set in gold to create the shape of the bee. 'I love bumblebees. You know I do.'

'So should I tell Sam to make the design?'

I found myself nodding.

'It'll take him a week or so to finish it, to buy the right diamonds and work with the gold instead of silver, but I'm confident he can do it. His silverwork is excellent. And it would give you time to decide what finger you'd like to wear it on.'

'I already know.'

He wrapped me in his strong embrace and kissed me. 'I'm sure I'll hear the cheering from the sewing bee ladies from here when you tell them the news.'

'I don't have to go,' I said.

'Yes, you do. Go and tell your friends, and they are good friends to both of us, that we're the ones getting married this year. You and me, Aurora. It's us.'

I wiped away tears of happiness, kissed him, picked up my bag and headed out.

I'd promised Ethel I'd give her a lift in my car because she had a lot of new yarns she wanted to show us. I parked outside her cottage and went in to help her carry the bags to the car.

'Thanks, Aurora. There's another bag over there beside the spinning wheel. If you wouldn't mind grabbing that for me,' said Ethel.

As I lifted it up, I noticed the framed photograph of Glen that usually sat in pride of place on the mantlepiece was now sitting on a high shelf where Ethel kept her ceramic ornament collection. The wedding photo had been added into the frame, and the pictures now sat where I thought they were particularly appropriate — next to a ceramic Highland cow.

The lights were on in Tavion's house as we drove up, and the door was open welcoming everyone in. I hadn't told Ethel my news. It was only a couple of minutes drive from her cottage to Tavion's house and I wanted to tell all the ladies together.

I carried Ethel's yarn inside to the living room. Tavion had helped them set up the sewing machines. He kept giving Tiree a loving glance as we sat down and got our sewing, knitting and craft work out.

Hilda frowned. 'Are you okay, Aurora? You look a wee bitty flushed.'

'I'm fine. Very fine, in fact. I have news for you all...'

When I told them in detail about the bee sketches, the ring design and Bredon's proposal, I knew that the postmaster down at the harbour would've heard the cheer never mind Bredon across the field.

'I understand that you want to take your time with your plans,' I said to Tiree. 'And you too, Mairead. You're far more sensible than me, but I want to grab the moment, to do this now, in the next few months. I feel it's right for me.'

Tiree and Mairead agreed.

'We're all different,' said Ethel. 'That's what makes us what we are.'

'This calls for champagne,' said Tavion. 'And phone Bredon. Tell him to get himself here so we can drink a toast to another happy couple.'

I phoned him. 'Be prepared to be smothered with kisses from well–wishers.'

'I'm on my way,' he said. He brought Sam, Fintry and the postmaster with him.

That evening, there was more chatter, champagne toasts and laughter than any actual sewing or knitting done.

As the night wore on, Sam went over and tried to turn the music on.

'It's eh...it's not working, Sam,' Tavion said, having nobbled it so we could have a jig–free evening.

'No worries, Tavion. I've got a blaster of a boogie box in my van. I'll bring it in and rig it up in minutes. Partner up and clear a space for the dancing.' He hurried out to his van.

There was a moment's lull followed by nods of approval. 'I could go another night of dancing,' said Bredon.

Fintry partnered up with Mairead. 'Suits me,' he said, giving her hug.

The postmaster held his hand out to Ethel and Hilda. 'One on each arm. What do you say, ladies?'

They put their quilting and knitting down and linked their arms through his.

Sam got the party going with some lively tunes. Everyone was up dancing, including Judith who enjoyed joining in with Bredon and Fintry.

As I headed to the kitchen for a glass of lemonade after dancing for a solid four songs in a row, I noticed a wee face peering in the patio window. 'There's Thimble.'

'Let him in, Aurora,' Tavion called over to me while doing a reel with the ladies. 'Give him a saucer of milk if he wants it.'

I slid the door open, and Thimble brushed himself against my leg purring. I put a saucer of milk down for him.

I drank my lemonade and then joined in again with the wild dancing. I pictured what the house would look like from a distance — all lit up, alive with dancing, music and friends celebrating — and the dressmaker's black cat slurping a saucer of milk while watching everything that was going on.


A few evenings later, after having dinner at Bredon's cottage, I popped up to my cottage to pick up some files filled with new features for the magazine. They included Mairead's illustrations and I wanted to work on them. I thought it would only take five minutes to get them and then head back down to the bee cottage.

The reaction to the magazine had been excellent. Sales were great and I was getting more subscribers every day.

I picked up what I needed and was about to leave when a man came walking along the road. At first glance I thought it was Sebastian. He was similar in age with brown hair, handsome face and wore a suit.

'Excuse me,' he said in a polite voice. 'Are you the owner of this cottage?'

'Yes, can I help you?'

He looked slightly lost. 'My car is parked down the road. I've been looking around the area.' He gazed up at the sky as if that was the most important view. 'I'm interested in your cottage. Is it available to lease?'

'Yes.' I'd been discussing leasing it out as a holiday cottage again. I planned to move in with Bredon. I sort of lived with him now. The cottage was empty most of the time. It seemed viable to rent it out.

'Perhaps I can drop by in the morning. I know it's late. I've been down at the harbour looking at the strawberry jam cottage. I believe it's available for lease too.'

'It is. The lease for it is dealt with by the dressmaker.'

'Yes, that's the lady I spoke to on the phone. She was very helpful. She advised me to have a look at both cottages and decide which one would suit me for my work.'

'And what type of work are you in?' I was being blatantly nosey but he didn't seem to mind.

'Stars. I'm a stargazer. I've been based in Falkirk for the past couple of years but I've been looking for somewhere else where the night sky is clear to view without the glow of urban lights blotting them out.' He again glanced up at the sky. It was clear, arching right along the coast, like a giant planetarium. Thousands of stars twinkled in the sky and the moon shone in the distance. 'You can even see Mars from here.'

'Can you?' I said, suddenly taking an interest in astronomy.

He point to a tiny dot along from the moon. 'That's Mars. Easily mistaken for a star but at this time of year you can view it with the naked eye. I'd of course set up my telescope. Do you have a loft conversation?'

'No.'

'No need.' He craned his neck back. 'The view from the garden here is magnificent, far better than the cottage at the harbour and it has a fine view.'

Then I realised something. I'd barely discussed my plan with Bredon to turn my cottage back into a holiday let. No one knew. No one except us.

'You said you spoke to the dressmaker and she definitely told you this cottage was for lease.'

'Yes. I was working in London at the time. That was about...oh...three weeks ago. I should've contacted you sooner but I've been so busy with work. I hoped the two cottage would still be available.'

'Three weeks ago?' I said thoughtfully.

100

He nodded and smiled, giving me a curious look.

I didn't tell him about the dressmaker. If he moved here he'd soon find out.

'I'll come back in the morning then?' he said, starting to walk away.

'Yes, I'm sure you'll like living here.'

He smiled and waved. 'See you tomorrow. I'm sorry, I don't know your name.'

'Aurora.'

His smile widened. 'Like the stars.'

I nodded and watched him walk away.

I glanced up at my cottage later on from the bedroom window as I lay snuggled up in Bredan's arms.

He kissed my brow. 'Looking at your cottage? Thinking of the past?'

'No, I'm thinking of the future.' My future with him at the beemaster's cottage where I truly felt I belonged. I'd told him about the man enquiring about the lease, and about the dressmaker. I cuddled into his chest, feeling the security of his arms around me, and looked at the cottage perched on the hill. 'It's never had a name, not like your cottage or Fintry's or even the strawberry jam one.'

'Do you want to give it a name?' he said.

I sighed and smiled. 'I think it's going to have a name.'

'And what name would that be?'

I kissed Bredon, knowing that my future was with him. I knew for sure. Marrying Bredon would be the right decision.

I kissed him again and then said, 'The stargazer's cottage.'

And then we snuggled up together and went to sleep. We had lots of plans for the future, including getting married in the autumn. Everything worked out the way it was meant to be. I'd found the man I belonged with — the beemaster.

End

Now that you've read the story, you can try your hand at colouring in the artwork designs and other craft projects mentioned in the book. You will find these on the book's accompanying website. Here is the link: http://www.de-annblack.com/bee

De-ann has been writing, sewing, knitting, quilting, gardening and creating art and designs since she was a little girl. Writing, dressmaking, knitting, quilting, embroidery, gardening, baking cakes and art and design have always been part of her world.

## About the Author:

Follow De-ann on Instagram @deann.black

De-ann Black is a bestselling author, scriptwriter and former newspaper journalist. She has over 80 books published. Romance, crime thrillers, espionage novels, action adventure. And children's books (non-fiction rocket science books and children's fiction). She became an Amazon All-Star author in 2014 and 2015.

She previously worked as a full-time newspaper journalist for several years. She had her own weekly columns in the press. This included being a motoring correspondent where she got to test drive cars every week for the press for three years.

Before being asked to work for the press, De-ann worked in magazine editorial writing everything from fashion features to social news. She was the marketing editor of a glossy magazine. She is also a professional artist and illustrator. Fabric design, dressmaking, sewing, knitting and fashion are part of her work.

Additionally, De-ann has always been interested in fitness, and was a fitness and bodybuilding champion, 100 metre runner and mountaineer. As a former N.A.B.B.A. Miss Scotland, she had a weekly fitness show on the radio that ran for over three years.

De-ann trained in Shukokai karate, boxing, kickboxing, Dayan Qigong and Jiu Jitsu. She is currently based in Scotland.

Her colouring books and embroidery design books are available in paperback. These include Floral Nature Embroidery Designs and Scottish Garden Embroidery Designs.

Also by De-ann Black (Romance, Action/Thrillers & Children's books). See her Amazon Author page or website for further details about her books, screenplays, illustrations, art and fabric designs. www.De-annBlack.com

**Romance books:**

Sewing, Crafts & Quilting series:
1. The Sewing Bee
2. The Sewing Shop

Quilting Bee & Tea Shop series:
1. The Quilting Bee
2. The Tea Shop by the Sea

Heather Park: Regency Romance

Snow Bells Haven series:
1. Snow Bells Christmas
2. Snow Bells Wedding

Summer Sewing Bee
Christmas Cake Chateau

Cottages, Cakes & Crafts series:
1. The Flower Hunter's Cottage
2. The Sewing Bee by the Sea
3. The Beemaster's Cottage
4. The Chocolatier's Cottage
5. The Bookshop by the Seaside
6. The Dressmaker's Cottage

Sewing, Knitting & Baking series:
1. The Tea Shop
2. The Sewing Bee & Afternoon Tea
3. The Christmas Knitting Bee
4. Champagne Chic Lemonade Money
5. The Vintage Sewing & Knitting Bee

The Tea Shop & Tearoom series:
1. The Christmas Tea Shop & Bakery
2. The Christmas Chocolatier
3. The Chocolate Cake Shop in New York at Christmas
4. The Bakery by the Seaside
5. Shed in the City

Tea Dress Shop series:
1. The Tea Dress Shop At Christmas
2. The Fairytale Tea Dress Shop In Edinburgh
3. The Vintage Tea Dress Shop In Summer

Christmas Romance series:
1. Christmas Romance in Paris.
2. Christmas Romance in Scotland.

Romance, Humour, Mischief series:
1. Oops! I'm the Paparazzi
2. Oops! I'm A Hollywood Agent
3. Oops! I'm A Secret Agent
4. Oops! I'm Up To Mischief

The Bitch-Proof Suit series:
1. The Bitch-Proof Suit
2. The Bitch-Proof Romance
3. The Bitch-Proof Bride

The Cure For Love
Dublin Girl
Why Are All The Good Guys Total Monsters?
I'm Holding Out For A Vampire Boyfriend

**Action/Thriller books:**
Love Him Forever
Someone Worse
Electric Shadows
The Strife Of Riley
Shadows Of Murder
Cast a Dark Shadow

**Children's books:**
Faeriefied
Secondhand Spooks
Poison-Wynd
Wormhole Wynd
Science Fashion
School For Aliens

**Colouring books:**
Flower Nature
Summer Garden
Spring Garden
Autumn Garden
Sea Dream
Festive Christmas
Christmas Garden
Christmas Theme
Flower Bee
Wild Garden
Faerie Garden Spring
Flower Hunter
Stargazer Space
Bee Garden
Scottish Garden Seasons

**Embroidery Design books:**
Floral Nature Embroidery Designs
Scottish Garden Embroidery Designs

Printed in Great Britain
by Amazon

36794353R00066